# Skye's the Limit!

Dream Big!

## BY MEGAN SHULL

For my parents

This book would not exist without two real live goddesses: Alice Saltonstall and Noni Korf Vidal. They are grace personified. Thanks also to my wonderfully bright editor Therese Kauchak; Will Capellaro; Lindsay Eisenhut; Leslie Daniels; the entire crew at Pleasant Company; and my agent at ICM, Richard Abate. Always warm thanks to my teachers, family, and friends, who inspire and bless.

Published by Pleasant Company Publications
Text copyright © 2003 by Megan Shull
Illustrations copyright © 2003 by Pleasant Company
Book Editor, Pleasant Company Publications,
8400 Fairway Place, P.O. Box 620998, Middleton, WI 53562.

CREDITS
Children biking © Royalty Free/CORBIS. Part of the poem "Ithaka"
appears on page 20. "Ithaka" was written by Greek poet
Constantine Cavafy in 1911.

SPECIAL THANKS
Paralympian Mike Crenshaw; Bill Coleman of Maryland Real Life
Designs; Lewis Glenn, Outward Bound USA; Ithaca FedEx; and
Robert and Betty Matyas.

Printed in the United States of America
03 04 05 06 07 RRD 10 9 8 7 6 5 4 3 2 1

**Library of Congress Cataloging-in-Publication Data**

Shull, Megan.
Skye's the limit! / by Megan Shull.
p. cm.
Summary: Eleven-year-old Skye O'Shea is homesick and afraid as
she sets out for a three-week bicycle adventure camp on British
Columbia's Cat Island, but despite a bully, mountains, and other
challenges she has the time of her life.
ISBN 1-58485-769-2
[1. Camps—Fiction. 2. Bicycles and bicycling—Fiction.
3. Interpersonal relations—Fiction. 4. Self-actualization—Fiction.
5. British Columbia—Fiction.] I. Title.
PZ7.S55942 Sk 2003      [Fic]—dc21      2003001218

# Let's Start with This

I am sitting on the bus, three rows back, sandwiched between Paige (my best friend) and Isabel (my neighbor). It's spring. It's sunny. It's the last day of school. We have no problem acting extremely silly. To top things off, I have just announced my top-secret summer plans.

"OK, wait. Let me get this straight," says Paige. She is looking at me like I'm crazy. "You're gonna fly in a plane, all by yourself, 3,000 miles away, to go to some adventure camp where you don't know *anybody?*" She pauses dramatically. "Aren't you, like, scared?"

"Well—" I start, but Isabel jumps in.

"You're *so* lucky, Skye," she says. "I have to babysit all summer!" Isabel shuts her eyes like she's dreaming. "Three whole weeks, riding bikes around an island in the Pacific Ocean. Toasting marshmallows every night over a campfire." She turns to me and smiles. "That is just so cool. *So. Cool.*"

Paige grins. "Are there going to be any *boys* on this island?"

We all crack up. Paige is a little boy crazy. I reach down, unzip my backpack, and fish out the official Cat Island Adventure Camp catalog so they can see for themselves. Paige flips through the photos of smiling campers. "Wow!

# Cat Island Adventure Camp

**Have the summer of your life!**

## Jump onto your mountain bike

and get ready for the ride of your life! Nestled off the coast of British Columbia, Canada, Cat Island is home to wildlife, hot springs, whitewater rapids, and the beautiful Sanchee River. On this odyssey you will loop around Cat Island on the newly restored Kingfisher Bike Trail, considered to be one of the most spectacular bike trails in the great Northwest. This trek offers 337 rolling, twisting miles of pure adrenaline adventure! For 21 days you'll sleep under the stars, cook over an open fire, and learn to live among your peers! Beginners welcome.

*Join our 21-day coed summer session for kids ages 11–14. Bikes, helmets, T-shirts, and shorts provided.*

SKYE O'SHEA
Fairway Drive
Ithaca NY 14850

"This looks fun!" she says. And it does.

When the bus comes to a complete stop at Kyle Kimber's brick driveway, Paige is still glued to the catalog. "Oh my gosh! It says you get to swim in the ocean," she reads out loud, "and sleep under the stars!"

I stand up, sling my backpack over my shoulders, and grab my language arts posters, my stuffed science notebook, and my balled-up gym clothes. Paige rolls up the catalog and sticks it under my arm. She is smiling at me.

"I just have one question for you," she says. I wait. I struggle to not drop all my stuff. "OK, if you're on an island in the middle of nowhere . . ." She pauses. "What do you do when you gotta *go?*" Isabel and I laugh all the way down the aisle and out of the bus. Paige yells out the bus window, "OK, I'm now officially jealous, Skye! Bye!" She waves.

"Bye, Paige!" we yell back. Isabel and I walk up the middle of the road to the row of mailboxes where our driveways meet. "So when do you leave?" she asks.

"In ten days," I say.

"Ten days! That's so soon!" says Isabel. "No hockey camp?"

"Yeah, well, my mom says I can only do one or the other, and this just sounds so . . ." I strain my brain for the right word. "So—"

"Glamorous," says Isabel.

"Exactly!" I say. *Glamorous*.

Isabel flashes me her megabuck smile. "You're gonna have a blast," she says. She turns away and starts walking up her driveway. "And I'll write, I promise!"

The minute I walk in the door, I sprint up to my room, dump my backpack on the floor, and call my mom at work. I am already picturing myself getting on the plane, and as soon as I hear her voice, I start talking. "Mom, I decided."

"Decided? Decided what, Skye?" she asks.

"Camp!" I tell her. "I'm going to Cat Island."

"Sweetheart, that's marvelous!" she says. "It's going to be such an adventure."

"I've got to send in the application, like, soon!" I say. I am panicked. *The application is due tomorrow, and now that I've told everyone, I mean—*

"Skye, calm down," says my mom. "Listen, I already checked with the Cat Island people, and we'll just mail the application with the check tomorrow. They said that's fine."

"Are you sure?" I ask.

"I'm sure."

"Really?"

"Really."

"Thanks, Mom," I say.

"Now, go clean your room. I saw it before I left for work, and it's a pigpen!"

After I hang up, I collapse on my bed. For a split second I wonder if I should change my mind. I've gone to the same hockey camp for the last five years. It's three miles from my house. It's a sure thing, a guaranteed good time. Plus, I know everybody there, and everybody knows me. This adventure camp thing—this is kind of crazy. It's like nothing I've ever done before.

My stomach flutters, like it knows this is a momentous decision. I hang off the side of my bed and grab the Cat Island catalog. "Have the summer of your life!" it says in bold writing. *The summer of my life,* I think, smiling, and I close my eyes. *The summer of my life.*

# The Next Morning

I splash water on my face, pull my hair back into a ponytail, and saunter downstairs in my favorite silky pink polka-dot pajamas. My mom is already up, sitting at the kitchen table, drinking her morning tea, and reading over the Cat Island catalog. She looks up, beaming. "I've been looking at your catalog," she says. "Biking around an entire island, camping under the stars . . ." She's really excited about this. Her eyes are twinkling. "This is going to be fabulous!" she says.

It takes me about an hour, but I fill out the three-page Cat Island Adventure Camp application, which includes a 200-word personal statement, a medical form, and this insurance thing my mom and I both have to sign. I read the insurance form out loud. "As a participant in Cat Island Adventure Camp, you hereby release CIAC, Inc., of any liability and assume any and all potential risks and dangers, including serious injury and *death*." *Gulp*.

My mom explains to me that this is just a precaution. "You'll be fine, sweetheart," she says between bites of the cheese omelet we are splitting.

# Cat Island Adventure Camp
## Personal Statement

In 200 words or less, tell us why you would like to attend Cat Island Adventure Camp. Please include a brief description of your previous biking or athletic experience. Describe your greatest strength and what you think will be your biggest challenge. Be specific! This information will help our staff get to know you better.

I have played hockey since I was five years old. I think my hockey background will help me be in good shape to bike around Cat Island, because you use a lot of the same muscles for hockey and biking. Hockey has helped me be a team player and learn how to work hard toward my goals. I think my biggest strength is that I think positively and am usually in a good mood. For me, the hardest thing about this adventure will probably be that I'm doing something I've never done before, and it's scary. Also, I'm not exactly Ms. Outdoors. Except for one overnight in Brownies when we slept in the Arnot Forest, I have never been camping. (Plus, you can't really count that, because in the middle of the night, it started raining really hard and we moved into a cabin.) So that's it. I really want to go, and I can't wait!

*Skye O'Shea*
Signature

Skye Beryl O'Shea
Print name

When I have answered every last question,
I fold the application, slip in the check from my
mom, and tuck them both into an extra-large
envelope. I put four stamps on the outside and
walk down our long driveway to the mailbox.
Maybe it's fate, maybe just coincidence, but right
as I get to the mailbox, the mailman drives up—
right at that very second. I'm not even
exaggerating.

"Hello there," he says, handing me a big
stack of mail, mostly catalogs and bills. I hand
him the thick Cat Island envelope in return.

"What do we have here?" he asks. He
holds my envelope up and examines it closely.
"Adventure camp, huh?"

I nod yes and squeeze out a nervous grin.

"British Columbia! Wow. That's a long way
from home."

"Ah, yeah. I know," I say.

"Good luck." The mailman sticks his arm out
the window and gives me a big thumbs-up. "I
bet this will be one summer you never forget!"

I sit down on the big stone fence, watch
the mail truck vanish into the distance, and look
up at the perfectly blue, sun-drenched sky.
I'm going. I'm really going, and there's no
turning back.

# Seventeen Hours Later

I'm turning back. *What in the world was I thinking?* It's two in the morning, and I'm lying in bed. This is the third time tonight that I have woken up in a cold sweat.

I toss. I turn. I pray. *Please let my application be lost in the mail.* I secretly swear to stop reading Laura Ingalls Wilder forever, never watch *Survivor* again, and give up my chances with every cute guy I'll ever have a crush on. But my little deals don't make any difference. Nobody is listening up there. Nobody is paying attention. The fact is, in exactly eight days I'm going three thousand miles away from home for three entire weeks, and this was all entirely *my idea!*

# Thirty Minutes Later

I throw off the covers, get out of bed, and maneuver around the piles of clothes scattered across my floor. I am whimpering. I'm sniffling. My nose is running. The house is pitch-black. I walk down the narrow hallway, my hands feeling the way, until I stumble into the closed door to my parents' bedroom. I turn the knob and walk in the darkness, following the sound of my dad snoring, until I clonk my knee on the edge of the wooden bed frame. (I do not recommend clonking your knee on a wooden bed frame.)

"Owww!" I yelp, hopping up and down on one leg and clutching my knee. My head hurts, my knee is throbbing, and big, wet tears are rolling down my cheeks. I'm a mess.

"Mom," I whisper. No answer. I shake her lightly. "Mom!" I shake her again, this time harder.

"Skye?" my mom finally mumbles.

"I don't want to go to adventure camp," I say in between sobs. "I can't . . ." (big breath) "I can't . . ." (tears) "I can't do it!" I finally get it out.

"Sweetheart, get ahold of yourself, please." My mom sits up in bed, searching for her glasses on the nightstand. "When you're crying like that, I can't understand a word you're saying."

"I don't want to go," I say, snorting and

wiping my nose with the back of my pajama sleeve. "Can you just call and cancel?"

"Nonsense," says my mom, "and please use a tissue, Skye. Don't use your sleeve." She turns to her nightstand, plucks a tissue out of the box, and hands it to me. I take it and blow my nose loud, like a foghorn.

She leans forward and strokes my cheek. "Sweetheart, you're just experiencing a very normal bout of jitters. Everyone gets nervous before trying something new. It's *normal*."

"But, Mom," I plead, "I can't go. I really can't. Seriously, you have to call them and ask for a refund."

She looks at me sympathetically. "Skye, honey, please try to get some sleep. You've sent the form in. It's too late. I wrote the check. Besides, we have lots to do. When we get you all packed, I know you'll feel loads better."

She takes off her glasses, places them back on the nightstand, and kisses me on the top of my forehead. "Everything will look better in the morning. I promise."

# Lucky Girl

My mom's right. There's something about the morning that just makes everything that was so scary seem like no big deal. I am feeling better. I am confident. *I can do this,* I tell myself.

After breakfast, my mom announces she is going to take the entire day off from work at the hospital to take me shopping. The plan is to make sure I have everything I need for camp. She sits down next to me at the kitchen table, and we go over Cat Island's official packing list item by item.

## 🚲 Cat Island Adventure Camp
### Packing List

*Bike, helmet, camp T-shirt, and shorts will be provided.*

- ❏ Headlamp
- ❏ Sleeping bag
- ❏ Sleeping pad (optional)
- ❏ Insect repellent
- ❏ Sunscreen (SPF 15 or higher)
- ❏ Shoes that can be worn in the water (1 pair)
- ❏ Pair of rugged sneakers
- ❏ Swimsuit (2)
- ❏ Rain suit (waterproof)
- ❏ Backpack
- ❏ Day pack
- ❏ Sun hat
- ❏ Towel
- ❏ Bandanna
- ❏ Water bottles
- ❏ Toiletry kit: toothbrush, toothpaste, soap, shampoo
- ❏ Sunglasses (optional)
- ❏ Underwear (six pairs)
- ❏ Girls: 2 sports bras— lightweight and fast-drying (optional)
- ❏ Nice outfit for the end-of-ride celebration dinner
- ❏ T-shirts (4)
- ❏ Shorts (2)
- ❏ Long pants
- ❏ Wind jacket
- ❏ Long-sleeved top
- ❏ Fleece top
- ❏ Handlebar dry bag for map
- ❏ Pajamas or sleepwear
- ❏ Mess kit

At the mall we lug around four gigantic shopping bags full of gear, clothes, and bike paraphernalia. "You are one very lucky girl," my mom tells me, pulling out her credit card at the sporting goods store. "Your sisters never got to do anything like this, Skye."

As soon as we enter the lingerie section of the department store, I look around to make sure I don't recognize anyone because, let's face it, it's totally embarrassing to be looking at a bunch of flimsy little pairs of underwear and lacy bras in public. I walk behind my mom, and after every few steps she turns and plops a bra into my hands. "You need support," she says. "All women do!"

I dodge behind a mannequin. "Shhh!" I say. I do not want to discuss my first bra with the entire store. But my mom is unfazed.

"This is a practical matter," she tells me. "You need something to wear as you're biking up those mountains!" She stops walking in front of the Ralph Lauren section, reaches into her purse, and pulls out the Cat Island packing list. "Lightweight and fast-drying sports bras," she reads out loud. "You could swim in these, too." She piles one more item onto the heap I'm carrying. I guess I roll my eyes or something, because my mom stops walking and turns to me. "Listen, Skye. I don't know why in the world you get so embarrassed about these things. It's natural! Now let's go try these on."

She follows me into the cramped dressing room and sinks into the chair in the corner. She looks at her watch and sighs. "We've been cooped up in this mall all day. Let's get moving!" She fans her face with the rolled-up list. I strip off my Lakeview Middle School T-shirt and take a bra off the clear plastic hanger. "This is going to be it!" says my mom, smiling at me. I slide the blue-and-pink stretchy elastic over my head and wiggle through the armholes. I stare admiringly at my reflection in the mirror and smile because, even though I wouldn't actually admit this to my mom, I think I kind of like wearing a bra. My mom stands behind me and adjusts the straps. "How does it feel?" she asks. She yanks down on the front until the wrinkles vanish.

"It's fine," I say, like it's so no big deal, even though I kind of think it is.

At the checkout counter, the saleslady helping us is an older woman with short silver hair. She smiles at me and then at my mom and rests her eyeglasses on the bridge of her nose. "What do we have here?" she asks, sorting through my pile. She holds up each pair of underwear and my two identical blue-and-pink bras. "Oh, my, these are adorable!" She inspects each of my items, folds them all neatly, and slips them into a white plastic bag. She leans over the counter and hands me the goods. "You're a young lady now, sweetie pie!"

# Farewell to Me

The night before I'm leaving we have a good-bye party. All nine of us fit perfectly around the long, narrow table at the back of the restaurant. My family is there, including my older sisters, my mom, and my dad. Of course, I have invited Isabel and Paige. To round out the list, there's my best friend from hockey, Apple, and Apple's mom, Summer. My dad jokes that this is my last night in civilization. "Tomorrow you might be eating dried grasshoppers cooked on skewers over an open fire!" he says.

My sister Shelby rubs her stomach. "Char-grilled grasshoppers. Yum!"

"Grasshoppers? I heard it was earthworms!" jokes my mom.

"No, *fried* earthworms," says Summer, winking at me.

So in honor of my last night in the modern world, I order pizza with black olives and a large Shirley Temple. While we wait for our dinner, the waiter brings three wicker baskets over-flowing with greasy French fries. We all dig in.

After fries, salad, pizza, three Shirley Temples, and strawberry rhubarb pie, I'm stuffed. Everybody is having a good time. It's some send-off. My sisters are even being nice to me. Shelby leans across the table and hands me a small blue silk bag that's cinched tight with a red string.

"This is from us," she says, nodding toward my other sister, Shannon, who's sitting next to me. They look at me eagerly. "Open it!" they say.

All eyes are on me. I unravel the knot, open the bag, reach in, and pull out a lucky arrowhead necklace, identical to the ones my sisters both wear. "Whoa! Thanks!" I say, and I mean it. I've always wanted a necklace just like theirs. My sisters are obviously pleased that I like it. They are smiling.

"We thought you might need a little extra luck on your adventure," says Shannon. "Put it on!" I slip the thin brown leather cord around my neck.

Shelby gets up out of her seat, moves to the back of my chair, and ties the ends of the cord together in a special square knot. It won't come off, even if I go swimming. "Don't lose it," she orders before flashing me a smile.

My gifts don't end there. Summer and Apple pass down a tiny box with an orange ribbon. The talking at the table quiets down and everybody watches me carefully undo the ribbon. "Just tear it off," says Shelby. But I take my time. Inside the box rests a tiny white feather and a smooth, small, round stone with a perfect hole in the middle.

"We found them at the lake," Apple explains. "My mom says they're lucky."

Summer leans over in her seat. "I think it's an owl feather," she explains. "Owl feathers are very auspicious. They bring you wisdom."

My mom reaches out to examine the fragile feather. "Wow. Gorgeous, Skye. That's really special." And it is. I tuck the feather and the rock back into the box and smile at everyone. I'm starting to get homesick and I haven't even left.

Isabel gets out of her seat and kneels down next to me. She's dressed in jeans, a T-shirt, and this cool straw cowgirl hat she got on her last trip to Brazil. "I didn't get you anything, but I thought you might like to take this with you." She reaches up, takes off her hat, and places it on my head. "You can give it back at the end of the summer," she tells me. Isabel shifts the hat around until it rests perfectly on the top of my head. I turn toward the windows that line our table and look at my reflection. The corners of the hat are turned up, and there's just enough room for my ponytail to hang out the back. It's so cool.

"Thanks!" I say.

"Lookin' good," replies Isabel, smiling back at me.

Paige passes down a white T-shirt that's rolled up and tied with a blue ribbon. "This is to give you special powers," she tells me. I unroll the shirt and shake it out in front of me. The words *Super Girl* are written across the front of the shirt in bold orange letters. It's very hip, very Paige, very cool. I decide on the spot to wear it to the airport for my flight tomorrow.

I fold up the T-shirt and start to stand when my dad catches my eye. "One more," he says, tossing an envelope at me from his end of the table. Nobody is paying attention anymore. Summer and my mom are deep in conversation. Apple, Isabel, and Paige are making a strange concoction involving salt, pepper, and melted vanilla ice cream. My sisters are flirting with the waiter.

I sit alone and open the envelope. Inside is a note from my parents, some blank postcards, and a bunch of Canadian stamps. I look down the empty table at my dad. He winks at me. "You can do it, kid," he says over the chatter.

We all get up and pose for a picture in front of the restaurant. My mom and dad stand in back of me, my sisters on each side, and Summer, Apple, Paige, and Isabel stand in the back row. Everyone's smiling, including me.

Dear Skye,

Tons and tons of love to you on your wonderful adventure! Remember, every great journey begins with one step. We are proud of you, sweetheart, for challenging yourself. Always keep your "thoughts raised high," your chin up, and your heart open! We love you!

Love, Mom and Dad
xoxoxo

"... Hope the voyage is a long one, full of adventure, full of discovery. Laistrygonians and Cyclops, angry Poseidon—don't be afraid of them: you'll never find things like that on your way as long as you keep your thoughts raised high, as long as a rare excitement stirs your spirit and your body ... May there be many a summer morning when, with what pleasure, what joy, you come into harbors seen for the first time ..."
—CONSTANTINE CAVAFY

# Flight

In the morning I wake up, shower, and dress. I slip on my new *Super Girl* T-shirt and my favorite pair of worn jeans with pink-ribbon piping down the sides, and I pull my hair back in a ponytail like I always do. I walk over to the full-length mirror that hangs on my closet door and carefully place Isabel's straw cowgirl hat on top of my head. I adjust it until it's tilting just right and wink back at my reflection. This is a thing I sometimes do that I would never admit to publicly—but I *do* look pretty cool.

My room is a mess. All the clothes I've decided not to take are in big heaps on the floor. My one regulation-size backpack sits on top of my bed, stuffed to the brim with my new bounty of gear, clothes, and enough bug spray, sunscreen, and shampoo to last me three summers, even though I'll only be gone three weeks. In a separate smaller, yellow day pack that Shannon lent me, I place my optional luxury items: a pen, one book, and a tiny airplane pillow I found in my mom's closet. I slip my lucky trinkets into the side pocket: the feather, the stone, and the postcards from my mom and dad. I zip the day pack tight, sling it over my shoulder, and carry both bags downstairs where my mom is waiting.

My dad already gave me a big pep talk before he left for work, and my sisters are at hockey camp. I sit down at the kitchen table and eat a bowl of cereal. I watch my mom throw a last-minute lunch together, in case I get hungry on the plane. "It's important for you to eat, Skye. You have to store up energy for your adventure," she tells me. She wraps up a peanut-butter-and-jelly sandwich in wax paper and puts it in a brown paper bag with three cookies, a bag of salt-and-vinegar chips, and a water bottle. "You've got a long day ahead of you, sweetheart," she says, handing it to me. "Don't forget to eat."

The ride to the airport is shorter than I want it to be. I'm nervous, my stomach is fluttering, and, to be honest, I'm feeling kind of sick. By the time we park and unload my two bags from the back of the car, my head is starting to heat up and my hands are sweaty. I think I'm having a heart attack. My mom looks over at me and smiles. I'm pretty sure she can tell I'm about to cry, and she doesn't want to make this any harder than it already is. She's acting like this is no big deal, like I fly on a plane by myself—to a place I've never been, to meet people I don't even know—all the time.

# Departure

In the airport, my mom waits with me. We sit by the big windows and look out at the plane. A small jet will take me to Pittsburgh, where I will board a big plane to Vancouver, where I will be met by the camp staff and the other campers who are flying in. Then we'll all pack into a van and drive to the ferry that will take us to Cat Island.

The thought of it all is overwhelming. I turn to my mom. "Are you sure I have to go?" I ask. "I think I might be coming down with something." But my mom just smiles. I look back at the entrance to the airport and picture myself darting out the door and running the entire way back to my warm bed. Instead, I lean over, hug my mom tightly, and try really hard not to cry.

"Listen, Skye. I know you can do this!" my mom says, hugging me back. "You are strong. You are wonderful. *You are going to have the time of your life!*"

"But what if I hate it?" I ask, tears trickling out of the corners of my eyes. "I mean, what if I don't make any friends, or what if I'm the worst biker in the world?" I look up at her. "This could be a total disaster!" I am now officially crying. My mom reaches into her purse and pulls out a pack of Kleenex.

"Here, sweetheart. Pull yourself together."

She hands me the Kleenex and strokes the hair out of my eyes. "Listen. Always remember, your father and I are thinking of you, and we love you. You are going to be just fine."

Before I can say anything, we are interrupted by a male voice booming over the loudspeaker. "Flight 711 to Pittsburgh now boarding, Gate 3. Flight 711 to Pittsburgh now boarding, Gate 3," repeats the voice. "Final call."

We stand up. I throw my arms around my mom. "Sweetheart, come on," she says, patting me on the back. "You will love it. I promise."

I let go, take a big breath, and wipe my eyes with the back of my hand. The flight attendant who's supposed to make sure I get on the right plane in Pittsburgh comes over and asks if I am ready to go. She's tall, blond, and gorgeous with a big, toothy smile. She introduces herself as Faith. I'm not kidding. That's her name: *Faith*. It even says so on the tag pinned to her blouse. Even I admit this is a good omen. *What are the chances that she'd have a name like that?* I think, as I turn away from my mom and walk with Faith out the door. We head down the steps to the boarding area and up the steep metal stairs to the plane's entrance. The propellers swirl the wind around us like a tornado. I hold the top of my cowgirl hat with one hand so it doesn't blow clear off my head. I turn around and look back at the airport window until I spot my mom waving wildly, and I blow her one last kiss.

# Pittsburgh

The flight from Ithaca to Pittsburgh is short and bumpy. I almost throw up three times, but by some miracle I don't. When we land, Faith grabs my arm. "We've gotta hustle," she says. I follow her down the aisle of the plane, down the metal steps, across the tarmac, and into the busy airport terminal. Inside the airport Faith hands me off to this tall redhead named Suzanne. "Good luck, hon," Faith tells me. "You're in good hands."

Suzanne informs me that we've got to hurry in order to make the next connection. We run the whole way until she stops by a sign that says Terminal C, where she hails one of those golf-cart thingies. "Jump on!" she shouts. We both hop onto the backseat, and this big dude with dreadlocks drives a zillion miles an hour.

"Don't you worry," he shouts, zooming through crowds of people, beeping loudly for them to get out of our path. "I'll get you there!"

At the gate, Suzanne bypasses the long line of passengers waiting to board the plane and introduces me to my next escort, Mia. Mia is tall with dark skin and pretty brown eyes. She looks through my tickets.

"Ithaca to Vancouver. Wow, that's a long trip," she says. She leads me through the metal double doors, down the vestibule, and onto the plane. "OK, you're in 3C—that's the aisle, third row back. Settle in," she says, pointing to my row. I sit down, tuck my day pack under the seat in front of me, and anxiously look around. I take out my little pack of tissues and blow my nose hard, tilting my head back and looking straight up at the ceiling, attempting to keep the welled-up tears inside my eyeballs. The air in the plane is stuffy, and it smells like jet fuel. I feel queasy. Dozens of passengers slowly cram the aisle next to me, stopping every so often to shove their carry-on luggage into the overhead compartments.

The two seats beside me stay empty until the last minute, when a young couple runs onto the plane and heads straight for my row.

"Hi there!" the woman says, scooting past me and smiling warmly. She has wavy black hair and a little diamond stud in her nose. She's really beautiful. I try not to stare.

"Excuse me," says the man with her, scooting past the woman and me to get to the window seat. I think he's her husband. They look like they're, you know, together. He is tall and dark, and they both look like pro athletes or marathon runners or supermodels. You know the type.

We all buckle our seat belts. I sit back and close my eyes. Saliva dances on my tongue. Stomach acid rolls up and down my throat. I think I might puke. *Great, just great,* I think to myself. *This is all I need right now.* I eye the white paper bag tucked into the pocket of the seat in front of me, close my eyes, and ask for some universal intervention.

*Don't throw up.*

*Don't throw up.*

*Please, please, PLEASE don't throw up!*

I say this over and over, silently, until I'm interrupted by a deep male voice—talking to *me*. It's Tan Man, in the window seat. He's leaning over his wife, asking me a question.

"Where ya headed?" he asks.

I look around to make sure he is talking to me, which is kind of stupid because he obviously is. "Ahh," I stammer, "adventure camp."

The Goddess speaks. "Adventure camp? Wow! That's awesome!" She grins. "Adventures are good for the soul."

*Uhhh . . . yeah. Good for the soul.* I smile politely and swallow hard, keeping the stomach acid at bay. The Goddess turns to me, her eyes open wide.

"So how long are you going for?" she asks.

*Swallow.*
*Breathe.*
*Don't throw up.*

"Ummm, three weeks," I tell her. "I'm biking on this old logging trail around an island off the coast of Vancouver. And . . ." I take a big breath—just saying it out loud makes it seem more real, like it's really happening. It *is* really happening. My stomach rumbles. I lean forward and turn to look at them both.

"I, ummm . . ." I pause right before I say it. I don't know what makes me do it, but for some reason I decide to admit to two total strangers that I'm scared—really scared—and nervous, and homesick already, and I'm not even there yet. "And I, ahh . . ." I try again. The Goddess and Tan Man are both facing me, waiting for me to spit it out.

"Well, I'm kind of apprehensive," I finally say. Yes, I actually use the word *apprehensive*. I have no idea where this word comes from. It just pops out of my mouth. "I've never been away from home before. I'm kind of scared about the whole thing," I add, holding back the tears that are fighting to spill out.

It's weird. As soon as I tell them that I'm nervous, my stomach stops churning and my forehead stops throbbing. I take a long, deep breath.

The Goddess turns and smiles at me. "I have a very strong feeling about this," she says. "Take a step toward fear, and the fear crumbles."

*Huh?* I don't really get it. I smile, though, because she's so nice.

"You are going to love it," she says, "positively love it!" She turns and looks me right in the eye, smiles, reaches out, and covers my hand with hers. Her hand is tan and strong, like she's a horse wrangler or a farmer or a rock climber. Her skin is rough and warm. Normally I would freak if a stranger just touched my hand because, first of all, it's a stranger. Second of all, I have this germ-phobia thing, and I don't like touching people I don't even know. But with The Goddess it's different. There's something kind of magical about her. It's like she's filling me up with courage. I sit for a while and don't speak.

The engines start up, and we taxi down the runway. The Goddess turns to me and shouts over the noisy engine, "There is nothing like adventure!" She reaches out and grasps Tan Man's hand, too. And the three of us, linked together in our row—me in my Super Girl shirt and cowgirl hat, my lucky necklace fastened tight—take off into the sky. And I just have this feeling that I'm going to be OK.

# Vancouver

My everything's-going-to-be-OK feeling kind of seeps out of me when we land.

"Have fun!" says Tan Man.

"You can do it," says The Goddess, winking before she turns and vanishes down the aisle. I stand in my empty row of seats and wait as everyone trickles past me. When the plane is empty, I walk down the aisle and meet Mia by the cockpit.

Mia walks quickly and I work to keep up as she dashes down the long hallway in the Vancouver airport. "OK, we're going to wait right here until your party meets you." She motions for me to wait by the window. I stand there and wait and read all the signs.

"Welcome to Vancouver International Airport," says the top sign. "Bienvenue! Aeroport International de Vancouver."

*Cool,* I think as I collapse into a chair. I have no idea who I'm looking for, so I just sit there— my day pack strapped over my shoulders, Isabel's cowgirl hat resting on my head, my heart beating a mile a minute—and wait.

# Cute Hat

I know the Cat Island people right off. It's that outdoorsy look—dead giveaway. The first one I notice is a tall woman in a light blue tank top. She's walking straight toward me. Maybe it's her smile, or her long dark hair, but something about her reminds me of Xena, the Warrior Princess. I like her immediately. Next to Xena is a strong-looking guy with honey-brown hair and a Cat Island T-shirt, just like the ones the kids were wearing in the catalog.

"Cute hat!" says Xena, before she goes to hug me—yes, *hug me*.

"You must be Skye!" says the guy, extending his hand for me to shake.

"Ah, yeah. That's me."

"T.J. Malone," he says, shaking my hand so hard, it hurts.

Xena thanks Mia, flashes her some identification, signs a piece of paper, and drapes her arm around my shoulders. "Let's go!" she says, and we all start walking toward the baggage claim. About halfway down the walkway, she stops cold in her tracks. "Oh my gosh! I completely forgot to introduce myself," she says, laughing. "I'm Tasha Daniels. I'm going to be one of your instructors."

When she tells me this, I feel immediate

relief. There's just something about her that's soothing. You just want to be near her or, if you didn't know her, you would wonder who she was. Plus, as soon as she walked up to me at the gate, I abandoned my plan to dash back onto the plane, hide in the cargo compartment, and head straight back home.

At the baggage claim area, T.J., Tasha, and I meet up with the rest of the group. I must be the last to arrive because everyone is waiting next to a big pile of backpacks and duffel bags. There are two other girls and three boys standing around, arms folded across their chests, staring at each other. Everyone looks older than me except for a couple of the boys.

T.J. lifts my heavy backpack off the conveyer belt. "Let's motivate!" he says, waving us on toward the airport exit. We all follow.

Outside, T.J. goes to get the van and we wait by the curb with Tasha. "Hey, why don't you introduce yourselves?" she suggests. I look at the two girls and three boys and smile shyly. I'm hoping someone else will break the ice, but nobody says a thing. Instead, we all just stand and stare at anything but each other. It is uncomfortable. Tasha finally steps in.

"OK, no worries. You're all a little shy on the

first day. I understand." She looks around at each of us with a twinkle in her eye. "I'll tell you what. I will introduce you." She points at me. "Skye O'Shea, Ithaca, New York!" she says, beaming. "Skye, this is . . ." Tasha turns and looks at the girl standing across from me. Her hair drapes around her face, and she's wearing all black, head to toe. Even her eyes are lined with thick black makeup. "Amanda McAdams from Berkeley, California?" asks Tasha.

But Amanda, if that's her name, doesn't say a word. She just glares at Tasha, rolls her eyes, exhales loudly, and slumps down on the linoleum floor, leaning her back up against the red Avis car-rental counter.

Tasha keeps going as if nothing happened. She turns to a small boy with round, gold-rimmed glasses and a navy blue T-shirt. "OK, help me out here. You are . . ." She squints her eyes as if she's thinking hard. "You are . . . oh, shoot. I'm going to get it. Wait a second. You are—"

"Charlie," he interrupts.

"Charlie Archer, of course!" says Tasha. "Charlie—Neenah, Wisconsin. Got it."

Tasha turns and looks at the girl standing next to Charlie. She looks to be about fourteen years old and has bleached-blond hair pulled loosely back into a ponytail. The girl speaks before Tasha has a chance to introduce her. "Merritt Medford. I'm from Lenox, Massachusetts, and, just so you know, I'm not here by my own choice." She turns away from us, storms over toward Amanda, and sinks down next to her.

*Oh boy. Strike two,* I think. I reach for my necklace and rub the arrowhead between my fingers, hoping very hard that there are some girls of the friendly variety waiting for me on Cat Island.

Tasha turns to the second boy, a tall, lanky kid with bad acne. "Ian Gaines, Toronto, Ontario, right?" she asks. He nods yes, scowls, and puts on the headphones hanging around his neck.

*Oh boy, this is getting better by the minute,* I think to myself. I turn my attention to the last boy left. He has a headful of black, curly hair and slate blue eyes that sparkle, even though we are standing in the shade. He looks a little like T.J. might have looked when he was twelve. There is clearly something different about him, something gentle and quiet, and—well, I'll just come right out and say it—*cute*. Really cute.

Tasha walks up to Blue Eyes. "And this is

Mason Grace." She pats his back. "He's the champ who helped me lug all the heavy gear bags to the curb."

With that, this beautiful creature called Mason Grace modestly lifts his head, looks up at me, and smiles. And with one grin—one little look—this boy who I don't even know, who I have never said a word to in my entire life, sends a little jolt right through my body, from the top of my head down to my toes.

# Frontsies

As soon as T.J. pulls the van up to the curb, Amanda McAdams and her new best friend, Merritt, call the first row of seats. "Don't even think about it, cowgirl!" says Amanda, scowling at me as I attempt to sit down beside her. I look back at her for one millisecond too long. "What are you looking at?" she snaps at me. "Do you have a problem?"

*Jeesh. Lovely. Off to a great start,* I think, climbing into the way-back row, trying not to have an all-out panic attack. Ian Gaines, his headphones still glued to his ears, helps himself to the entire second row. He sprawls his gangly body lengthwise and props his head against his bag, taking up the whole seat. Charlie climbs over the first two rows and squeezes into the seat next to mine, and Mason files in last, sitting down next to Charlie. The three of us are crammed together in the back row.

We drive out of the airport and onto the interstate, settling in for our four-hour journey. Nobody talks. The only sounds come from T.J., who is driving, and Tasha, who is sitting beside him in the passenger seat, holding a map and navigating. The ride is bumpy and stuffy and, since I'm crammed into the very back seat, it takes only a few minutes for me to feel hot and woozy. I prop both my legs up, rest my knees against the seat in front of me, and close my eyes. I tell myself everything's going to be OK, that I'm going to have fun, that this was my idea. I think about the catalog pictures of the ocean, the bikes, and the smiling faces that made me temporarily insane enough to choose *this* over hockey camp. And then, by the grace of God, I fall asleep.

# Candlelight

"Rise and shine, Skye." It's Tasha. She is shaking my arm. "Hey. We're here," she says. I look up, startled. It's pitch-black outside. Amazingly, I have managed to sleep the entire four hours, all the way through the drive and the ferry ride to Cat Island. Not as amazingly, I wake up with drool hanging off my front lip. *Cool, Skye. Real cool*, I think, wiping the saliva on my shirt and hoping Mason hasn't been watching me sleep.

But Mason isn't there—neither is Charlie or anyone else. I slip outside the van and look around. We are on a dirt road next to a sign that says *Kingfisher Bay*. Up ahead, a dim light glows on top of a hill. I pick up my packs and sleeping bag and start walking toward the light. I am so tired that I don't have any energy to be nervous. I can hardly remember where I am, let alone what I'm doing. I walk like a zombie.

"Long day, huh?" asks Tasha. She reaches out and takes the heavy backpack off my shoulders. "Here, let me help you with that," she says.

"Are you sure?" I ask, just to be polite.

"Go ahead. I've got it." She swings both my packs over her shoulder. "Why don't you hustle up and join the rest of the gang."

"Seriously?"

"Seriously." She smiles.

"Thanks," I say, even though I want to say more. I run up the hill toward the light.

"Have fun, Skye!" she shouts after me.

# Lucky

At the top of the hill, in a clearing by a small wooden cabin, sit three long picnic tables pushed together. Each is covered with a white sheet and a row of yellow candles that glow brightly. Everyone is already sitting down eating. There are more kids here, more than were in our van, and I search up and down both sides of the picnic tables for a place to sit. That's when I hear him. I don't know if it's my lucky necklace, the stone, the owl feather, or just plain old luck. It's Mason. He's talking to *me*.

"Hey, Skye, you can sit here," he says, scooting over to make room.

"Thanks," I reply. I climb over the narrow wooden bench and sit down next to him.

Mason shovels a forkful of food into his mouth and points to the cabin. "The food is over there," he says, chewing. "That's a cool necklace, by the way."

"Ahh, thanks" is all that comes out.

Mason nods, smiles, and turns to talk to the boy across from him. I sit shoulder to shoulder with Mason and wonder if this is all actually happening to me or if I'm in the middle of some strange parallel universe. Out of nowhere, T.J. appears and hands me a heaping plate of macaroni and cheese, stir-fried vegetables, and two brownies.

"Here you go, pal," he says.

Food. I'm starving. I totally forgot about the lunch my mom packed me, and I haven't eaten since breakfast in Ithaca. I dig in, treating myself to a brownie first. I listen to the conversations around me. To my right is Mason, who is still talking to the kid across from him. To my left is a girl who wasn't in our van. She looks nice, in the way you can tell that someone is nice by just looking at her. She's wiry and small, with jet-black hair that's pulled back in a ponytail just like mine.

I turn to her and smile. She smiles. I have to swallow my brownie before I can say anything, but she beats me to the punch.

"Hey, I'm Zoë—table-tennis champion of Minneapolis, Minnesota, and, yes, I am half-Korean and half-not, if you are wondering, because most people want to ask but don't." She tells me this in one big breath and laughs a deep, throaty laugh that seems funny coming from her rail-thin body. "I'm thirteen and three-quarters. What about you?" she asks.

"Twelve," I answer, but I do not volunteer that I've only been twelve for seventeen days. There's something about Zoë I like right away—maybe it's her fiery eyes or the fact that she's so funny. Whatever. All I know is that for those few seconds that she is laughing, I completely forget that I want to go home. I feel normal. And I know she will be my friend.

Zoë waves across the table at the tall, lanky girl across from us. She has stringy light blond hair, and a billion tiny freckles cover her cheeks.

"That's Pearl," she says. Pearl smiles at the introduction and reaches over a candle to shake my hand. "Hey, nice to meet you. What's your name?" she asks.

"Skye," I say.

"Cool name," says Zoë.

"Skye. That *is* cool," agrees Pearl. "Very chic," she adds, giggling.

For the first time since I met Tasha in the airport, I feel safe and calm. I feel like I might actually like this island. I might actually make it. And, as we eat and talk and laugh, I make sure to reach up and rub my lucky necklace—because whatever I do, I don't want my luck to end.

# Anywhere but Here

My good luck ends right after dinner, when
Amanda McAdams "volunteers" Pearl, Zoë, and
me to do the dishes. When the counselor asks for
volunteers, Amanda points to us. "Oh, you guys
want to do them?" she says, smiling devilishly.
"OK, that's cool. We can do them tomorrow!"

*Huh?* I think.

"Say what?" Pearl mutters.

But before any of us can protest, Amanda
grabs Merritt's hand and starts walking away.
"Night!" she shouts. And the two of them, along
with two other girls I have yet to meet, run all
the way up the hill.

The three of us watch in disbelief as the
four bodies disappear up the hill. "What's *her*
problem?" asks Pearl.

"That girl has issues!" says Zoë. And with this
we all crack up, because it's the one thing we
have all been thinking but nobody wanted to say.

You might think it's no big deal to wash all
those dishes, until I mention the tiny fact that we
are in the middle of *nowhere*. There's no sink
and no plumbing; the only running water is
Kingfisher Bay, about three billion miles away
from the back of the cabin. T.J. walks with us
down to the bay and helps us fill two metal
buckets with water.

"It's OK if you see a little dirt floating in there. We're going to boil it first," he explains. He carries one bucket all by himself, while the three of us struggle with the other bucket. Half of our water splashes over the edge. We place the two buckets on the ground by the fire. The tables are abandoned now. The only sign that anyone was even here is the big stack of dirty dishes. Everyone else has gone to the sleeping area: the girls on top of a hill to the right of the cabin, the boys up the dirt road by the woods. Apparently the camp director still isn't back from picking up the last lone camper at the airport, and the counselors decide they will save our big welcome-to-Cat-Island speech for the morning.

After T.J. boils the water and pours it into the three tubs he has set up on the table, we form an assembly line. Pearl's first. She squirts some soap into her tub, scrubs the gunk off a plate with a sponge, and hands the plate over to me. My job's easy. I rinse the soap off the plate in clean water and hand it to Zoë, who dips it into the stinky bleach solution. We continue washing until all the plates, cups, and silverware are done. T.J. stands at the end of the line and supervises. "Scrub 'em good," he tells us. "You want to get all the particles and bacteria off."

"Yum," says Pearl. "I love bacteria!"

"Yeah, bacteria and fried, crusty old germs!" adds Zoë, and we all crack up.

When we're done, T.J. helps us put everything away and points us toward the second hill to the girls' area. "Now go catch some shut-eye!" he says.

The three of us trudge up hill number two, backpacks and sleeping bags in tow. "Whoa!" Pearl shouts, stumbling as she feels her way through the darkness. "I can't see a thing! I'm blind as a bat!" We are so tired that everything we say seems hilarious, and we giggle uncontrollably as the three of us feel our way through the pitch-black night.

By the time we get to the top of the hill, my eyes have adjusted to the dark. I look all around me for a cabin like the one we ate by, or a rustic lodge with big wooden beds like you see in movies about summer camp. But as I look out into the dark, it slowly sinks in: no cabin, no lodge, no bed. I see nothing but a big field with knee-high grass and prickly weeds. My stomach starts to rumble. My hands are clammy. The darkness makes everything seem spooky and creepy, and there are strange animal-sounding noises coming from the woods. The three of us stumble on until we hear something, and I almost jump out of my skin.

"Hey," whispers a voice.

We stop in our tracks. I grab Pearl's arm and try not to scream.

"Girls! Over here!"

Pearl stays calm. "It's Tasha," she whispers. "She's over there." Pearl points toward the woods at a dimly flashing beam of light. We walk toward the light until we reach Tasha, who's sitting up in her sleeping bag in front of a small tent.

"Hey, thanks for cleaning up. The other girls are asleep already." She speaks softly and nods toward the tent. "You guys can either set up a tent or enjoy this gorgeous summer night out here, under the stars, with me."

I am so tired, so exhausted, that I can't really think straight. Plus I'm starting to feel a wave of homesickness. Fifteen hours ago I was home. *Home*. And now I'm about to sleep on the ground, in the middle of a field, on an island in the middle of nowhere!

Pearl turns to me and shrugs her shoulders. "I'm sleeping out here." She throws her stuff down in a pile a few feet from Tasha, rolls out her sleeping bag, and crawls in. Zoë and I follow suit. I don't change, brush my teeth, wash my face, or do anything I'd normally do before going to bed. I just worm my way into the long, narrow bag that I got at the mall six days ago and squirm around uncomfortably until I don't feel rocks jabbing me underneath.

The three of us lie side by side, wrapped up tightly under the enormous dark sky. The stillness of the night creeps over me. I shut my eyes and try to block out the fact that I really, really, really still wish I was home, safe and sound, worrying about nothing but who I want to instant message, or what I'm going to watch on TV, or if my mom will let me go to the mall.

*Twenty-one days? How will I last?* I think.

"Sweet dreams," whispers Tasha.

"Yeah, sweet dreams," mumbles Pearl.

"Good night," says Zoë.

"Night," I whisper back and wriggle into the hard ground.

# I'm Leaving

I do not sleep. I toss. I turn. I've never been so homesick in my entire life. And no matter how hard I try not to, all I can think about is how much I miss everyone—even my sisters. I miss my mom and my dad. I miss having everyone just know me and like me without even having to try.

I flip onto my stomach and smush my face into my pillow. I'm desperate. I'm having a nervous breakdown. I want out. This was the stupidest idea I ever had. I take big, deep breaths and exhale loudly on purpose, hoping someone will hear me, wake up, and make me feel better. I look at Zoë sleeping peacefully beside me, wrapped up in her orange sleeping bag, and stop just short of poking her so that she will wake up and save me.

*Breathe, Skye.*
*Breathe.*
*Breathe.*

I sit up and look over at my backpack. That's when it hits me. The answer is so obvious that I don't know why it took me this long to figure it out. I will leave in the morning. It's as simple as that. If I leave tomorrow I can be at hockey camp by the end of the week. The moment I decide this, my heart stops aching. I slither out of my sleeping bag, tiptoe to my backpack, and lug it closer to my sleeping bag. I'll leave in the morning.

"Skye?" It's Tasha. "Hey, everything OK?" she asks, squatting down beside me.

"Ummm, yeah," I say. I want to tell her that I'm leaving, to tell her, "Thanks for everything, but I have to go." But before I can say anything, tears flood my eyes.

Tasha puts her finger up to her mouth. "Shhh," she says. She stands up and motions for me to follow her.

It's hard to see when you're crying, but I manage to follow her, all the while snorting back the snot that's dripping from my nose. I glance back at the rest of the girls, hoping nobody is awake to witness what a big baby I really am.

"Shhh," whispers Tasha again, reaching out her hand to lead me. I follow the dim beam of her headlamp down the hill, past the cabin, to the edge of the bay. At the water's edge, I let go of Tasha's hand and sit down beside her. I wipe my eyes with the back of my hand. I sniffle back my runny nose. I take a deep breath and try to get a grip, but it's useless. My crying isn't pretty. It's that ugly kind of crying, and I can't stop. I take big, gasping breaths.

"Shhh, it's OK," Tasha says, her hand still resting on my back. "Your family must be pretty special."

I nod and wonder why I have never really realized this before. They *are* special. I'm lucky.

Tasha turns to me. "You wouldn't believe how homesick I was my freshman year of college." She shakes her head and smiles.

I stare at her. It's hard to imagine Tasha homesick. She's so strong and sure of herself— everything I'm not.

"Seriously!" she says. "It's true. After my parents dropped me off, I cried for three days straight. No lie. I can't describe it, except to say it was like I walked around with this knot in my stomach, and, no matter what I did, every now and then this absolute gush of sadness would sweep over me, and I would remember how far away I was from everyone."

I nod. "Yeah, I know," I say. And it's weird. There's something about telling someone how you feel that makes everything better. It's like you're letting the bad stuff out of your body and making room for light.

Tasha interrupts my daze. "Hey, you're gonna make it, Skye," she says, turning to me with a wide smile on her face. "I have *no* doubt!"

I shrug my shoulders. Maybe she's right.

Plus, if I left now, everybody at home would think I was such a loser. I don't want to have to explain to everyone I know why I didn't do what I said I was going to do.

Tasha jumps to her feet. "You know what?" she asks, extending her hand to pull me up. "In three weeks you're going to think this trip was *amazing*."

"Yeah, right," I laugh. I'm having a hard time imagining ever feeling that way. We start the walk back up the hill. "I'm serious, Skye. You watch," says Tasha, shaking her finger at me.

"Whatever," I reply, smiling.

"You'll see," she says. "You'll see."

# Fake It Till You Make It

I am an excellent actress. The next morning,
I smile and cheer and joke like I'm having the
time of my life. You would never know I'm
homesick. I am extra polite. I giggle. I kid around.
I help Pearl and Zoë wrap up their sleeping
bags, and I skip (yes, *skip!*) with them to breakfast, like there is no place else I'd rather be.

"This is going to be a blast!" says Zoë,
throwing her arms around our shoulders.

"Totally!" says Pearl.

"I know!" I say, turning to them with my
best, brightest smile. And I hope, soon, I'll
believe it.

At the cabin, T.J. assigns everyone different
chores. Pearl, Zoë, and I carry heavy logs from
the woods and place them in a circle around the
fire. Tasha and a bunch of other kids collect more
wood and add it to the blaze, until the flames are
orange and hot. Another group helps in the cabin,
mixing the pancake batter and washing blue-
berries. Everyone is so busy that no one really
notices when Merritt and Amanda stumble down
from camp, slither past the busy workers, and
flop down by the campfire. *Ugh,* I think. I don't
say anything, though. Mostly I just try to avoid
eye contact, because I really don't want to get on
anyone's bad side. I have twenty days to go.

T.J. squats by the fire, cooking up blueberry pancakes on a flat griddle. We sit around him in a circle, devouring every last morsel, until a tall man with a big white beard, a mop of silver hair, and a mustache sort of like Santa Claus's appears on the porch of the cabin. He strikes a metal cowbell, and the high-pitched clang gets everyone's attention. We all look up.

"Welcome, campers!" bellows Santa Claus. "My name is Harold Payson, otherwise known as Moondog, Chief, or The King." Everyone laughs. "Heck, you can call me Your Majesty!" More nervous laughter. Moondog keeps talking. "Today will be a day of preparation for our trek around Cat Island. We will get to know each other, learn to trust each other, and study the challenge that lies ahead." He pauses to clear his throat.

I glance at Merritt and Amanda, who are sitting next to each other by the roaring fire. They are busy whispering back and forth, completely ignoring Moondog's inaugural address.

"It will be challenging at times—pitching a tent in a different spot every night, not getting to shower, washing your clothes by hand," says Moondog.

*Gulp.* My heart beats faster by the minute.

Moondog goes on. "But it will also be, undeniably, the best time you've ever had in your life." I glance at Zoë. She smiles back at me. "What I need," says Moondog, "is cooperation." He repeats the last word, pronouncing every syllable: *"Co-op-er-a-tion!* That, my friends, is our word of the day."

After breakfast we split into two groups. The boys go with T.J. and this other counselor to unload their bikes, and we hike to a clearing in the woods and go over basic safety rules for our journey. Then, after lunch, the two groups switch. We unload our special Cat Island Adventure Camp mountain bikes from a musty yellow shed, learn how to change a flat tire, and take our bikes out for a spin around base camp. I pass Mason only when our groups cross after lunch. He smiles, I smile, this weird sensation flashes through my bod, and I attempt with all my might to not let my look linger.

# Dinner

We are back at the cabin. I am slicing carrots, Pearl is peeling potatoes, and Zoë is down by the bay getting more water with T.J. and some other kids. I carefully chop the carrots on the small wooden cutting board. I am ravenously hungry, and every so often I pop a slice of carrot into my mouth.

That's when I hear it: a high-pitched voice— a sneering voice, a not-very-nice-sounding voice.

"Excuse me," the voice says.

I turn around. Standing before me is a counselor with cropped blond hair and a nose that tips up at the end like a skateboard ramp. "Excuse me, but we need to save those for everyone else," she says, staring at me and nodding toward the carrots. She looks a little like Peter Pan, except she's a girl and she has blond hair. And she's mean.

"Ahh . . . oh, right. Sorry," I say, my stomach knotting, my face turning red. I positively hate getting in trouble—it's just this thing about me. I take a big breath and try with all my might to keep my bottom lip from quivering. Peter Pan turns around and walks out the door.

The second she leaves, Pearl laughs. "Give me a break," she says. "It's only a carrot. Big deal!" She looks around to make sure the coast is clear, grabs a carrot, and bites off a big hunk. I can't help but laugh, and her mischievous smile makes me feel instantly better.

After we finish our duties in the cabin, T.J. and the other guy counselor, Brad, tell us we are free to rest. They take all our chopped-up stuff—along with onions, cheese, and a rack filled with spices—out to the fire, where Tasha has set up a mini outdoor kitchen on an old card table. T.J., Brad, Tasha, and Peter Pan (who I hear other people calling Katrina) go to work on a masterpiece meal.

I sit back and watch T.J. stir all the ingredients into this giant wok set up over the fire. Whatever it is, it smells *so* good. I'm starving. I have three servings of the mystery concoction and two brownies for dessert. Food has never tasted so good. We sit by the fire on the very logs that we collected, split, and arranged in a circle around the campfire this morning. Everyone is present and accounted for. There are seventeen of us: seven girls, five boys, four counselors, and Moondog.

By nightfall the bonfire is raging. Brad walks over to the cabin, disappears for a few seconds, and reappears with a guitar hanging from a woven cloth strap around his neck. "All right, you guys," he says. "You're in for a treat." As Brad strums on the guitar, the other counselors hand out pieces of paper, and within minutes we launch into our first rendition of the Cat Island Camp Song.

**The Cat Island Camp Song**

Cat Island stars shine.
Cat Island beauty stops time.
Be brave, have courage, stand strong.
Never doubt or think your way is long.

Believe in your dreams and you will see
Courage, compassion, self-reliance set you free.

Over the mountains we go,
Over the mountains we go.
Grit, determination, and struggle
Make victory sweet and double.

Believe in your dreams and you will see
Courage, compassion, self-reliance set you free!

Cat Island stars shine.
Cat Island—always mine.

We sing it again and again, each time louder. We're laughing, enjoying the end of the day and being silly. After round three, I hear Amanda not-so-softly whisper to Merritt beside her. "Get me out of here!" she says, loud enough to make half the camp look over at her. She nods at Ian, and the three of them boldly stand up and walk behind the cabin. I watch as Moondog quietly slips away, too.

After four rounds of the camp song, Tasha stands up, her arms stretching over her head. "We need to get to know one another," she announces. "We've been so busy, we haven't made time for a serious get-to-know-you game." Everybody groans collectively. I look next to me at Pearl, who's listening attentively to Tasha, and then over at Zoë, whose shoulders are back, her face glowing as usual. I sit up straight and lean back against my log. I try very hard to listen and have a good attitude. After all, *cooperation* is the word of the day. Plus, Mason is sitting directly across from me. Every so often, if I lean back on my log just right, I catch his eye and we smile.

Tasha starts. She is sitting between Mason and Charlie, straight across from me. "Here's the deal. Are you ready?" she asks. We all nod yes. "I'll start us off. I'm going to say my name, an adjective describing me that starts with the first letter of my name, and then something I brought from home that's meaningful to me." There are a few murmurs and some nervous shuffling.

Tasha goes first. "OK, my name is—" she stops abruptly and looks up toward the four people walking back into the circle. Moondog leads the way, followed by Amanda, Merritt, and Ian. None of them look too happy, and I can only assume they all got a big-time talking-to by The King of Cat Island. Pearl nudges my leg with her elbow. I don't even have to look at her to know she is enjoying this little mishap. Zoë leans over. "Karma," she whispers. "That should teach Ms. Thing to tone down her royal-highness attitude."

# Mmmmajorly Hot

The three bandits and The King sit down at the only empty logs left around the circle. Moondog sits between Ian and Merritt, and Amanda sits next to Katrina, who I have been avoiding looking at since the carrot incident.

Tasha starts over. "OK, I'll explain this again for the latecomers. We are saying our names, an adjective describing ourselves that starts with the first letter of our first names, and something meaningful that we brought from home."

Tasha closes her eyes. She looks like a regal Egyptian queen. With her legs folded and her posture perfect, she leans back gracefully and takes a big breath, inhaling deeply through her nose. You can see her chest rise and fill with air. As she exhales, she opens her eyes like everything is fresh and new, and it feels like we aren't supposed to be anywhere else in the world but here.

"My name is Tasha. I am *tough*," she says and looks over at T.J., who returns her smile with a wink. "I brought this from home," says Tasha, reaching into her pocket and pulling out what looks like an old silver pocket watch. She holds it up and opens the fragile cover. "This is my grandmother's compass," she explains. "My grandmother was a fantastic explorer. She was one of the first women to circumnavigate the globe, and she was one of the greatest female sailors of her time."

"Awesome," says Pearl.

"Nice," says T.J. Everyone leans in to get a closer look.

Tasha hands the compass to Mason to pass around. "Very cool," he says, holding it in his hand and examining it more closely. That, as I am sure you can understand, makes me like him even more.

Tasha looks right at me. "Yeah, it's really special to me because when my grandmother gave it to me, she told me, 'Remember, there is never a road you can't travel, never a path you can't traverse. Always live for your dreams, and dream of the way you'd like to live. And do it!'" Tasha smiles broadly, and something about her just now reminds me of The Goddess from the plane. She's just so confident and joyful, and, I don't know, *positive*.

Mason is next. He passes the compass to the boy next to him and clears his throat like he's nervous. Everyone is staring at him. "I'm Mason," he says bashfully. "And, ahh," he stalls, scrunching up his face like he is thinking hard.

"And I'm *mmmmajorly* hot!" Pearl whispers.

I poke her in the gut with my elbow. "Shhh," I plead, trying not to laugh.

Mason is still thinking. We all wait. "OK," he finally says. "I'm Mason, and I am magical!"

"Ahhh. Interesting!" says Tasha.

"Please tell us of your ways!" jokes Katrina, moving her hands around like she is casting a spell.

Mason reaches into his pocket and pulls out a small leather-bound journal. "This is my journal. I always keep it with me—*always*," he says, emphasizing the *always*, as if to tell anyone who is planning on taking it that they don't have a chance. "I even sleep with it next to me." He pauses and turns to Tasha. "That's it, I guess." And with that he shoves the journal back into his pocket, looks at me, and grins.

# Whoa

Mason's smile sends my brain to some other planet, and I have to strain to concentrate on the next seven people.

Charlie, *creative*.

T.J., *tenacious*.

Becca, *brainy*.

Zack, *zany*.

Peter, *perfect*.

Caitlin, *caring*.

Ian, *idiot*. Whoops, I mean *individual*. I couldn't resist.

Next comes Pearl. She's sitting right beside me. I turn my body toward her and smile. She clears her throat and takes a deep breath.

"OK," she says, smiling back at me. "My name is Pearl, and . . ." she pauses, "and I am positive." And then, all in one motion, she reaches down, pulls up the right side of her sweatpants, and *takes off her leg!*

Yes, you read that right. I said her *leg. Her leg!* She takes off her leg and holds it in her hand. From her knee down she doesn't have a leg. No leg. Nothing. Nada. Zilch. Everyone gasps, including me. I mean, you just don't expect someone to take off her *leg.*

Pearl holds up her leg with her right hand. But it's not a real leg; it's a thin black rod with a sneaker attached to the foot. Pearl is smiling. She doesn't look as nervous as she did before her turn. She's more relaxed, like the cat's out of the bag, like it's a relief to show us all her big secret. She looks over at Tasha and smiles. Tasha smiles back and gives her the thumbs-up sign. I get the feeling that Tasha has known all along.

I turn to Zoë. We both have our eyebrows raised in surprise, and our mouths are hanging wide open. Then I look back at Pearl, still sitting next to me, still holding up her leg.

"OK, as you can see, this is my leg!" she says proudly. Everybody kind of laughs, but in a good way, not like they are making fun of her. It's just surprising to see someone holding up her leg. "So here's the story, and I am only going to tell it once, so listen up."

A hush comes over the circle. Even Ian looks captivated.

"OK, so three years ago, when I was ten years old, I was with my mom driving to my soccer game. It was, like, four in the afternoon, in the middle of the summer, and—" she pauses.

I lean forward. *And what?*

"—a drunk driver hit us. Head-on," Pearl adds.

For a few lingering seconds there is dead silence. The only sound comes from the fire, crackling and snapping in front of us.

"Yeah, I know. It was awful," says Pearl, finally breaking the tension. She is relaxed. You can tell she has told this story many times before. "But the thing is, we were really lucky. My mom and I both lived. The guy that hit us is dead."

More silence.

More fire crackling.

Zoë glances over at me. Her eyes are as wide as mine are.

"As you can see, I lost my leg from the knee down. They had to amputate." I look at her knee. A thin white cotton sleeve, sort of like a tube sock, is slipped over the stub. She looks around the circle—at Tasha, and even at Merritt and Amanda. You can tell that everyone is captivated by Pearl and her story. There's just something about her that makes you instantly love her.

"Um, so anyway, I'm what's called a *below-the-knee amputee*, or BK for short," says Pearl. "And two months after the accident, I learned to walk again on this special prosthetic leg. It's made of carbon fiber. It's pretty high-tech." She holds her leg up again so we can all see. "And I've been running and jumping and biking—and just about anything else you can dream of—ever since. Most people can't even tell I'm any different."

Pearl smiles broadly. Everyone is still staring in disbelief.

"To take it off, I just push this button, and *voila!*" She puts her leg on and takes it off a couple of times to show us. "You'll be seeing me take it off a lot, because I don't swim or sleep with it on." Pearl looks around the group and smiles. "So anyway, I guess that's why this—" she holds her leg in both hands like a prized possession "—is really my all-time favorite object. It gives me freedom, and it's taught me that I can do anything anyone else can do—sometimes more."

Pearl snaps her leg back on, locking it into place. She rolls her pant leg back down, crosses her legs, and sits up straight. "And if anyone has any questions about my leg or anything, just ask me. I'm happy to talk about it. I just don't like people talking behind my back." She turns to me, puts her arm around my neck, and leans over. "Bet that's a tough act to follow!" she says, squeezing my shoulder as if to signal I can do it. And that gives me just the courage I need.

# Cowgirl Kryptonite

It's my turn. I take a deep breath and get a nose full of smoke from the fire mixed in with my own ripe body odor. I reach up and rub the arrowhead dangling around my neck and hope something comes to me, because I have no idea what I am about to say. "Ummm," I say, starting off the way every other kid before me has. "My name is Skye O'Shea, and I am . . . I am . . ."

I look over at Pearl and then at Zoë, as if they can telepathically help me think of something smart and funny and cute to say. But they just smile back.

"My name is Skye," I try again. "And I am . . ." Everyone starts to shuffle impatiently. I look down at the shirt I've been wearing for the last two days. "Super Girl!" I blurt out. I blurt it out and smile because, I mean, *Super Girl?*

T.J. hollers from across the way, "So what did you bring with you, Super Girl?"

Before I can answer, Amanda jumps in. "Hey, cowgirl. Did you bring some kryptonite?" She bursts into laughter and looks at Ian and Merritt who, by the smirks on their faces, obviously think I'm one big joke.

For a few seconds, everything goes into slow motion, and I start to notice I can't even look Amanda straight in the eyes. She gives me the creeps, and when she looks at me, I feel kind of stupid. It's like I need to somehow be cooler or more stylish, or speak some secret language that only cool people know.

Pearl nudges me in the gut. "Skye," she whispers.

I snap out of it and turn my attention back to the rest of the group, which is still waiting to hear what I brought from home. Without really thinking about it, I raise my arm and feel around my neck until my fingers find the thin leather cord.

"I brought this necklace," I say, holding up my arrowhead for everyone to see. "It's an arrowhead." I am careful not to look toward Amanda. "It's lucky," I say. Right about now, with Amanda McAdams and her little posse snickering at me, I am hoping that it is.

# The Next Morning

Moondog is standing in front of the cabin ringing the cowbell. He strikes it three times. "Round up!" he roars, waving one hand over his head, motioning everyone to gather around him.

I have wolfed down breakfast, washed my mess kit, and placed my packed bags and rolled-up sleeping bag by the van as instructed. T.J. explained to us last night that this is how it will be each day as we make our way around Cat Island, sleeping in a different spot each night. Each morning we'll load our sleeping bags and packs into the van, and Moondog will drive the van to meet us at the next spot. That way we don't have to bike with all the extra weight of our gear.

Like everyone else, I'm decked out in Cat Island Adventure Camp clothes head to toe— black soccer-style shorts, a light blue T-shirt, and a fluorescent yellow camp-issued helmet. Well, actually, none of the others have their helmets on yet, but I try mine on for size. I buckle the black strap under my chin and sneak a glance over at Mason, who's leaning against his bike. He nods back at me with a bashful smile.

Mason's little grin is about the only good thing that's happened since I woke up in my sleeping bag before sunrise. My stomach is upset, and I've had to sprint into the woods two times, squatting down in the high grass and hoping nobody sneaks up on me doing my business. At the risk of sharing too much information, I would like to point out that I have officially run out of tissues from the little pack my mom gave me at the airport, and I have resorted to using a leaf to—well, *you know.*

I sit down on the grass and look at the crowd and at Moondog, who's still waiting for everyone to settle down. Pearl and Zoë wheel their bikes up to me, lay them down on the grass, and sit down beside me. Just like everyone else, Pearl has on her black shorts, her shiny, ultra-modern prosthetic leg in clear view. It's hard not to stare at it. It's pretty cool. Zoë is busy coating her face with thick white sunscreen. "Want some?" she asks. I reach out, and she squeezes a big glob into the palm of my hand.

I am smearing sunscreen all over my face and neck when Moondog gets started. "Welcome to day three!" he says loudly, over the chatter of campers. A hush comes over the group. Even Amanda, standing by the door to the cabin, stops talking and looks up. She has abandoned her usual black attire for the light blue camp T-shirt, except she and Merritt have both cut off the sleeves and cropped the bottoms, effectively transforming them into tank-top belly shirts.

Pearl leans over. "Check out the Siamese twins!" she says, amused. And maybe I'd be amused, if Amanda didn't scare me half to death and gnaw a hole through my stomach every time she looks at me. Instead, I just turn my attention to Moondog.

"Today is a very significant day in your life as a Cat Island adventurer!" he says. "Today is the day we set forth on our journey!" Everybody cheers nervously. Moondog turns to T.J. "I'm handing it off to T.J., who is going to let you know what group you are in."

*What group I'm in? What does he mean, what group I'm in?*

Everyone must be thinking the same thing, because it gets real quiet, fast.

T.J. walks up the steps to stand next to Moondog. T.J. is adorable and sweet. It's easy for us to listen to anything he has to say. "OK! Y'all ready for a great day?" he asks.

"Yeah!" we shout.

"Here's the deal. We'll all be eating together and camping together at night—boys in one sleeping area, girls in another. But this year we're doing something a little differently than we have in years past. We're going to split everyone up and ride with separate coed teams for the entire duration of this journey."

"Coed teams?" Zoë whispers. "Sounds good to me!"

Moondog raises his voice. "When the teams are announced, I don't want to hear any complaints. They are set for a reason, and they aren't going to change." He takes off his big straw hat and wipes his forehead with a tattered red bandanna. "Any questions?" he asks.

Nobody says a word.

T.J. has the floor again. He holds up his clipboard. "I'm going to read off this list," he explains. "If you are on the list, you're with Katrina and Brad. If I don't call your name, you're with Tasha and me."

I look down, shut both my eyes, and cross every one of my fingers—and my thumbs.

"If you hear your name, head on over there." T.J. points to Katrina and Brad, who wave their hands high over their heads and smile. I grab the arrowhead around my neck and start rubbing hard, like it's a magic lamp.

*Don't say my name.*

*Don't say my name.*

*Don't say my name.*

T.J. clears his throat. "OK, here goes. Group one: Amanda . . ."

*Oh no! Please, not me.*

Pearl glances at me. I can tell by the look in

her eyes that she is thinking the same thing.

"Caitlin, Peter . . ."

*Please no.*

*Please no.*

*Please no.*

"Becca, Ian        "

*One more.*

*One more.*

*One more, and I'm home free.*

"And . . ." T.J. stalls, scrunches up his eyebrows, and whispers something to Moondog. "And Merritt," he says.

"Yes!" shouts Merritt, pumping both her fists in the air.

But trust me, nobody, and I mean *nobody*, is as happy as I am.

# Fun

Pearl, Zoë, Mason, Charlie, this other boy, Zack, and I gather around T.J. and Tasha on the sunny side of the base-camp cabin. Zack is small and delicate. His hair is blond and sticks up in every direction. He sits down next to Mason and Charlie, and all three boys lean back against the side of the cabin. Zoë, Pearl, and I sprawl out on the grass alongside them.

Tasha sits down in front of us, next to T.J. "We have quite the crew!" she says.

"Don't I know it!" T.J. replies, squinting into the glare of the sun.

Zoë leans over. "He is so cute!" she whispers. I keep my eyes on T.J. and try not to crack up.

"All right, guys and gals," T.J. continues. "We're going to be doing some serious bonding on this journey." He pauses and looks around the group. "And to be honest, there are going to be times when we will be under a lot of stress. We're really going to need to support each other, especially when the going gets tough." I peek over at Mason, Charlie, and Zack.

T.J. turns to Tasha and then back to us. "One thing we have to really be certain we take care of," he says, "and we mean this seriously—"

"It can be summed up in two words," says Tasha. "Any idea what they are?"

Mason repositions himself, flipping onto his stomach and propping his head up with his hands. The other boys follow suit. Nobody seems to want to talk first. Charlie finally breaks the silence. "Bike safely?" he offers tentatively.

Tasha smiles at Charlie but shakes her head no. "Well, that's important, too, but that's not it," she says.

"Be considerate?" says Zack.

"Another good one!" Tasha answers. "But still not what I'm looking for." She looks back at us and waits patiently.

"Um, I know!" announces Pearl. "Encourage each other?"

"That's a good one, too. Three words, though, darlin'!" Tasha says, laughing. We all laugh, too.

"Eat often?" jokes Mason. More giggling.

"Don't quit?" shouts Zoë, cracking up.

"Rest frequently?" I ask, joining in. We all are laughing, even T.J. and Tasha.

"The answer is," Tasha turns to T.J. and they say it together, "have FUN!"

# The Route

It takes awhile for us to settle down and stop laughing, but when T.J. pulls out his clipboard, he means business. "Let's talk about our mission," he says.

"As you know, our goal isn't to cover just part of this island," he smiles. "Nope. We're here for the whole shebang. We'll be biking around the entire perimeter of Cat Island." He takes a stack of small sheets of paper off his clipboard and hands one to each of us. "This should give you a good idea of what we're in for."

I hold the map in my hands and stare at it blankly. My stomach does a little flutter. The island looks bigger than I thought it was, and there are a lot of little mountains drawn in.

"This is the route we'll be taking," T.J. says. He holds up the map and points to the route. "I strongly recommend keeping the map in the dry bag attached to your handlebars at all times." T.J. points to the trail with his finger. "As you can see here, we'll be following an old logging trail that loops around the island. It's called the Kingfisher Bike Trail, and it's one of the most scenic bike trails I've ever been on. We're in for a real adventure."

Tasha jumps in. "Since the trail follows the edge of the island, we get to swim every night.

It's so gorgeous." You can't help but believe her.

T.J. holds up the map. "This map is going to come in very handy when we're in the middle of the woods or if we get lost in the mountains."

*Middle of the woods? Lost in the mountains? What?* The risk-acknowledgment form flashes through my head, and my forehead gets sweaty. I reach up to push the hair out of my eyes and discover that I have been wearing my fluorescent-yellow bike helmet this entire time! Mortified, I unbuckle the clip under my chin and strip the helmet off my head. I peek over at Mason, but he's not even looking at me. He's looking at Tasha, who's holding up her grandmother's compass.

"We'll all get a chance to practice some navigating," she assures us.

*Great. Navigating.* I glance nervously at Pearl and then Zoë for a little sympathy. But neither of them looks the least bit nervous. If anything, they seem raring to go, eager to jump on their bikes. So when Pearl looks back at me, her eyes wide with excitement, and mouths, "This is so cool!" I muster up my courage and smile back.

T.J. clears his throat. "There's one thing Tasha and I really want to stress. This is not,

I repeat *not*, a race with the other group." When T.J. says "the other group," we all turn and look at Katrina, Brad, and their team sitting under a gigantic willow tree near the woods. "We really need to be on the same page on this one, guys," T.J. adds, looking each of us in the eyes. "Competition just ruins everything. So even if they egg us on—and they might—" he looks at us totally seriously, "stay cool, OK?"

"And be safe," adds Tasha.

"Group hug!" T.J. shouts. We all pile together until we are a giant heap of tangled bodies on the ground, laughing. And right then I start to feel like this might actually be kind of fun.

# Seven Hours Later

Did I say fun? I'm riding in a complete downpour, every ounce of me soaked to the bone. "Did I actually sign up for this?" I mutter to myself. I shout the same thing to Pearl, who is biking behind me. "Did we sign up for this?" I scream.

"What?" she shouts back. It's practically impossible to hear through this rain.

"Where the heck is the van?" I yell, turning back so she can hear me.

"What? Did you say something?" Pearl yells.

I try again. I take a deep breath and shout as loud as I can. "WHERE'S THE VAN?"

"Huh?" she screeches back. "If you're talking to me, Skye, I can't hear a word you're saying!"

Snot is dripping down my chin. I watch as it falls onto my leg. Gross. Balancing my handlebars with one hand, I wipe away the dirt on my forehead with the back of my arm. If this weren't actually me, it might be funny. But it *is* me, and the sun is going down and I'm starting to freeze. My teeth chatter as I pedal against the wind and rain. Tasha, the three boys, and Zoë are all so far ahead of us that they appear in the distance as tiny specks. I can barely see them. The road ahead is winding, narrow, and washed over with mud. According to our trusty map,

the old-fashioned railroad car we are sleeping in
tonight is seven miles ahead.

I move my legs around and around, pushing
down on the pedals as hard as I can. I dream of
a hot shower and a warm meal, and I turn to
look back at Pearl and T.J. bringing up the rear.

After a good two miles of wind and torrential
rain, I give up. I steer to the side of the road and
set my bike down in the ditch. Pearl and T.J. pull
over behind me.

"You OK?" shouts T.J. through the downpour.

I wipe my wet hair out of my face. "Isn't
there a van or something that's gonna pick us
up?" I ask, shouting back.

He holds up his walkie-talkie, encased safely
in a waterproof bag. "If you really can't make it,
I could radio back to Moondog in the van. Do
you want to stop?" he shouts.

"Stop?" says Pearl, looking at me like I'm a
Martian. "Heck, no! It's only rain. We're not
going to melt!" She turns and looks at me. "Do
*you* wanna stop?" asks Pearl, like the thought
has never occurred to her. She reaches over and
grabs both my shoulders and shakes me. "We
can do this, Skye!" And even though muddy, wet
drips are streaming down her face, and her hair
is sticking out every which way, she is smiling.
I think she's actually having fun. "Trust me!

Come on!" she says, waving for me to follow her. And with that, she climbs back on her bike, throws her leg over the top bar, and pedals away.

T.J. and I stand there, and for a split second I think about packing it in, quitting, and calling it a day. I think about waiting with T.J. at that very spot for Moondog to rescue me, my stupid bike, and my soaking-wet body from this miserable, flooded mess.

T.J. holds up the walkie-talkie. "Hey, do you want me to call?" he asks again. Every ounce of me wants to stop, lie down on the side of the road, and quit. But when I look up the path at Pearl riding through the rain, halfway out of sight, some strange supernatural force moves through my body. And the next thing I know, I'm hopping on my bike and pedaling as hard as I can.

# Drip Dry

The railroad car is no four-star hotel, but it's warm and dry, and there's a roaring fire in the corner woodstove. I walk dripping wet into the room that has a "Girls Only!" sign taped to the outside of the door. Pearl and Caitlin are still changing. I nod hello to both of them, collapse onto the floor, and peel off my waterlogged clothes. A couple of days ago, I would have been embarrassed to completely change clothes in front of other people, but I'm so wet and tired, I don't even care anymore. I take off everything— my shirt, shorts, underwear, sports bra, socks, and sneakers—until I'm stark naked. I pull a towel out of my gear bag and dry off, then stand up and slip into my cozy pink pajamas. I pile everything into one big, wet heap, carry it with me back into the main room, wring out my clothes on the front steps, and lay them all in front of the fire.

From the looks of it, I'm the last to arrive. Everyone else is in pajamas (girls) or sweat suits (boys), with the exception of Amanda. She has changed into her black outfit and has even applied eyeliner and red lipstick. It is clear that Brad and Katrina's group arrived way ahead of ours. "Nice of you to help out," Amanda snarls at me as I walk past.

*Huh?* I think, confused. I mean, I just got here! I look at the table, set up with a big pot of spaghetti, a plate of meatballs, and a dish of tofu arranged neatly in a row.

When I walk up for a closer look, Katrina appears in front of me. "Skye, you need to make sure that you help clean all this up when you're through," she says, pointing toward the pots and pans piled in a tub in the makeshift kitchen.

"Um, OK," I say, a little confused at what she is talking about. *Isn't it kind of obvious that I just got here?* I think, shooting a look at Pearl. Pearl is equally baffled by Katrina's unfriendly nature. She shrugs and makes a sympathetic face.

"Hey, listen, folks. We cooked. You clean," Katrina tells us, pointing to her group and then to ours.

I try not to roll my eyes as my mom's voice rings in my head: *Be polite, Skye. Be gracious.* So I just look away from Katrina's glare, turn toward Pearl, and line up for food with the rest of my team.

T.J. stands behind the steaming food and piles the provisions high onto each of our plates. Charlie pops a meatball into his mouth. "I'm starving!" he says, his mouth full of food.

"So am I!" says Zoë, slurping up a piece of spaghetti.

"There's nothing like eating after working hard," says T.J., chomping on the garlic bread. I stuff a forkful of food into my mouth and nod in agreement.

And it's weird. Even though all seventeen of us are supposedly riding together, it is completely obvious that a division has been made, and the camp has splintered in two, right down the middle of the old railroad car. Katrina, Amanda, Merritt, Ian, and their posse are giggling to themselves in front of the fire, and our team is off to the side, leaning against the worn maple-paneled wall.

# One Day Later

The rain has cleared. It is sunny and hot, and there's not a cloud in the sky. We are only ten miles into our ride when I hear it: a scream.

"Help! Help!"

It's Pearl! I throw my bike down on the pavement and run back around the bend in the trail. Mason, Zoë, Zack, and Charlie are already kneeling down next to Pearl. T.J. is standing about ten feet away, talking into his walkie-talkie.

"We'll find it, I promise," Tasha tells Pearl.

I kneel down next to Zoë. She leans over and whispers in my ear. "This tiny little bolt that keeps the screw tight for her leg slipped off," she says. "We can't find it anywhere."

I look around at my team. Everybody looks bummed, frustrated that there's nothing we can do. Mason stands up and waves us over. "Let's spread out and see if we can find it."

I follow everyone else, looking straight down at the pavement and studying the path. That's when I first hear it: whooping and hollering. I look up, just in time to jump out of the way of Amanda whizzing by me on her bike. She almost smashes into Pearl. The rest of Amanda's group follows close behind.

"You snooze, you lose!" shouts Amanda as she passes me.

"What a jerk!" mutters Charlie.

"She is so rude!" says Zoë.

"Hey, Brad, Kat—get your posse to slow down!" shouts T.J. into his walkie-talkie. He's mad. I look over at Mason as he watches Amanda and her crew disappear into the distance. His eyes are on fire and, for a split second, I think he might blast off and run after them. Instead he turns his attention back to the ground and the missing piece.

The five of us backtrack, walking slowly with our eyes peeled for the bolt. About halfway down the trail, Mason lies down on his stomach, presses his ear flat to the pavement, and squints like he's watching ants crawl. "Wait!" he shouts. "Don't move. Nobody move!" We all freeze. Mason jumps up, sprints about ten yards down the trail, squats down, and picks up a tiny little bolt. "Found it!" he shouts, waving the very small piece above his head and racing back at us down the trail.

Pearl breaks out her tools from her handlebar bag, pulls out a small wrench, and goes to work tightening the bolt. She locks her leg back into place and springs back up on her feet. "What are we waiting for? Let's go!" she says. Like eight ducks in a row, our team rides out together, zooming down the narrow path and shooting down the other side of the hill.

# Four Days Later

I wake up smelling like I haven't showered in days, which is true. The dirt on my face rubbed off onto my white pillowcase last night, which strikes me as kind of disgusting. We slept in an abandoned farmhouse that had no running water, no beds, and no mattresses. But it was warm and dry and more comfortable than the ground outside. I sneak out while everyone is still asleep. I grab my soap, towel, and toothpaste, throw them into the little red bucket that T.J. brought for us, and head down the hill toward Snow Goose Bay.

It's still kind of dark out. The sun isn't quite all the way up yet, and the air is cool and sharp. It's eerie. It takes me awhile to get my bearings and figure out where the path is. I keep walking farther and farther down the hill, until I can hear the water lapping against the shore. The morning light is just peeking through the mountains. I throw my stuff down, sit on the damp grass beside the shore, and dangle my feet in the icy water. I look up toward the rising sun. I think about how I'm not even really that homesick anymore. I think about how it's pretty cool to wash your face right in your own private bay, with the sun rising in front of you, the birds singing, and the morning air fanning your face.

I think about how I'm kind of liking this outdoor, roughing-it thing.

And then it happens. I am kneeling down beside the water, toothpaste still in my mouth, rinsing the last bit of dirt and grime off my face, when she sneaks up on me.

"Skye," I hear.

I hear it, and I wish I don't. I wish it were just my imagination. I wish it were really a bird, or the wind, or anything except for what I know it obviously is. Amanda.

As soon as I register her voice, my stomach drops. The air gets heavy. My heart thumps so loudly that I can hear it outside my body. I stand there, my face still dripping wet, frozen in place.

Amanda is not smiling. "I want to talk to you," she demands. She sounds weird and mad and hostile. My heart is pounding louder than before. I can just tell something bad is going to happen, because my body has this alarm system for people who are going to hurt me, and it's going off like the fire alarm at school, except the sirens are inside my head.

*Vacate the premises.*

*Leave the building.*

*Exit quickly and in an orderly fashion!*

*Danger ahead!*

I stand like a statue, unable to move. I wish

really hard for Pearl to come skipping down the hill or for Tasha to magically appear. But when I close my eyes, turn my head, and spit the toothpaste out of my mouth, I look up and Amanda is still there. She's standing in front of me, a little too close for comfort.

"Ummm," I say, stalling for a bright idea, stalling for a way to escape this moment, hoping I'm just hallucinating, but I know I'm not.

"Can we talk later? I have to go get my bike ready," I say. It's lame, I know, but I say it. I'm desperate. This does not cut it with Amanda.

"Look," she says, shoving her face into mine, "you always want to get out of everything, Skye. It's so annoying. It's just one of the many things I hate about you."

*What?* I look at her like she's crazy.

She just keeps spewing over. "Obviously you hate me. Obviously we are *enemies*!" she says. I look around me to make sure this is actually happening, that it's not just some bad dream. I'm hoping that maybe I'm actually still asleep, back up in the farmhouse on top of the hill.

Amanda is not done. She shoves her finger up against my collarbone, poking me. "Look, Ms. Skye O'Shea, or Super Girl, or whatever your stupid name is." I take a step back, but Amanda comes toward me. She raises her voice. "Let's just decide to be enemies, because you are annoying and ugly and stupid, and you drive me crazy with your little I'm-so-great act, because you're really *not!*"

*Don't cry. Don't cry. Don't cry,* I think. Tears temporarily stall at the edge of my eyes. I try to calm her down. "Look," I say, choking on my heart, which happens to be jammed someplace halfway up my throat. "I don't know what you're talking about. I don't have anything against you, Amanda. Maybe this is some misunderstanding," I say.

This just gets her even madder. "Sure, some *misunderstanding*," says Amanda, her face two inches from mine. "Here's the misunder-standing—" She is shouting now, and I am really hoping that someone—anyone— hears her and comes to rescue me, or stick up for me, or drag her off of me. I glance up the vacant hill toward the farmhouse. Amanda sticks her finger up to my face. "The only misunderstanding here is YOU," she says, her spit sprinkling my nose and cheeks. "I'm sick of you! Consider yourself warned, Super Girl!"

Amanda reaches out and rips my necklace off my neck. It happens so fast, I don't have time to fight back. The cord breaks off easily; the knot must have been loose. I watch in

shock as Amanda McAdams, with my lucky
necklace tucked away in her hand, turns around
and struts back up the hill.

# One Minute Later

I am crying the kind of crying that makes
you short of breath—that makes your eyes red
and your nose run. I'm trembling. Even though
it was just words, my body, my head, my
stomach, *everything* hurts.

I sit slumped on a rock beside the water, my
elbows on my knees, my face in my hands, my
palms pushed up against my eyes. I search my
brain for something that I did or said to make
Amanda so mad at me. I play everything back in
my head like a movie: the first day at the airport,
the van ride to Cat Island, that whole doing-the-
dishes thing. But no matter what, I still can't
figure out why she hates me so much.

I stand up, step down into the shallow edge
of the bay, bend over, and scrub my face again.
I scrub hard and long, until I'm sure there's no
trace of Amanda's venom on my skin. Then I
empty the red bucket of my stuff, fill it up with
water, and pour it over my head. I do this once,
then again and again, until my scalp tingles from
the chill of the water and my brain feels clean.

I step out of the water onto a warm flat rock,
sit back, and look out at Snow Goose Bay. Just
beyond the bend I can see a tall ship with
flowing white sails gliding across the water.
I watch the ship sail away from the island and

seriously consider ditching everyone, swimming out to the boat, and hoisting myself aboard. I wish I could just leave this crazy scene and these crazy people and go home.

# Five Minutes Later

I'm not that good a swimmer. I would never make it to the boat, and, to tell you the truth, it kind of freaks me out that I have seriously considered this as an option. I mean, really, I'd never make it in a million years. Who am I kidding?

All I know is that for the first time in my life, I feel this type of miserable that I've never felt before. It's like I'm just numb, and a part of me that I came here with is gone. I don't even really feel like myself anymore. I'm starting to think Amanda didn't just steal my necklace. She stole *me*.

"Skye!" Zoë is shouting. I can see the faint outline of her figure at the very top of the hill. "Skye! Where are you?" she yells, her voice getting louder as she bounds down the hill. "Hey, what are you doing down here? I've been looking all over for you."

I look up with the best fake smile I can muster and tell myself to say something funny and friendly and normal, and just skip over the part about the fight. But it's too obvious to hide. My eyes are all red and puffy. I can't just pretend nothing happened.

When I tell Zoë about my run-in with Amanda, she looks at me like she can't believe it. "Give me a break!" she says, shaking her head back and forth. "Obviously she's jealous of you, Skye."

*Jealous? Of me?* I look at Zoë like she's crazy.

"Let's face it. You're funny and charming, and everyone can't help but fall in love with you!" Zoë says this all very convincingly. "You're everything she's not. Duuuuh!" She laughs. "Besides, as I believe I have already mentioned, that girl has some serious *issues!*" And for the first time since Amanda purged herself on me, I laugh, too.

When Pearl comes down the hill to find us, I tell the story again. "Oh my gosh!" says Pearl. "We should really tell Tasha." But I don't want to tell Tasha. I mean, then I'd be a tattletale. Plus, I would like to do everything and anything to forget this stupid little incident even happened.

"Let's just forget about it," I say, half-trying to convince myself and half-trying to convince the two of them.

"OK, Super Girl," agrees Pearl. "We won't say anything to Tasha or T.J., but I still really think you should. Someone needs to stop that big bully or she's just going to do it again. But it's up to you." She shrugs her shoulders and smiles.

Zoë leans over and puts her arms around me.

"Group hug!" she says. As I'm sandwiched between the two of them, a little piece of me comes back to life, like I'm a dried-out sponge and they just added water. I can breathe again.

# Three Hours Later

I don't feel better for too much longer.
I manage to get two flat tires in a row: one by
the switchback mountain pass, where a zillion
pinecones devour my front tire, and one over
by the lake where we all stop for lunch.

"Wow! You are having a tough day!" T.J.
tells me as I struggle to fill my tires back up
with the pump. "Hang in there, Skye. Your luck
will change."

But let's face it. A certain thing is missing
from around my neck, and it's pretty clear all
my good luck went with it.

# Seven Hours Later

I have avoided *you know who* all day. I do not look at Amanda at breakfast. I do not walk by her at lunch. I do not stand anywhere near her or her friends at dinner. I tiptoe around her like she's a tiger, ready to pounce. After dinner, I even get to the tent early to make sure my sleeping bag is farthest away from hers. I avoid her at all costs. The only place I see her—the only place she keeps turning up—is at night when I shut my eyes and try to go to sleep, and all I can think about is her.

# One Day Later

I'm at mile seventeen of Bear Mountain Pass, pulled over on the side of the road, when Katrina catches up to me. I am alone. In my dumb move of the day, I told Pearl and Zoë to go on ahead, that I'd catch up. I should have known better. Katrina and Tasha switched groups today.

Katrina lays her bike down beside mine and stands next to me on the rocky edge of the road. She is smiling this weird fake smile, and there is something about her that makes my personal-safety alarm buzz.

"How ya doin', Skye?" she asks, but she doesn't wait for me to answer. "Listen, I heard you had a little run-in with Amanda."

*What? How does she know?* "Ahh—" I say, stalling. *Who told her?*

Katrina takes a big swig of water before she says another word. I stand there waiting for the ball to drop. I start to have a seriously uneasy feeling. Big drips of salty sweat roll down my forehead and neck, soaking through my shirt.

Katrina finally speaks. "Look, she told me all about it, Skye." Katrina sighs this fake sigh. "To tell you the truth, I am really disappointed that you have not taken the initiative to work things out with her."

*What? I haven't taken the initiative? What is she talking about?*

My brain churns in overdrive to figure out how this thing with Amanda is somehow *my* fault.

"Yeah, well . . ." There are a million things I want to say.

*What about my necklace?*

*What did I do?*

*How can you not see through Amanda?*

*How can anyone not tell how mean and horrible that girl is?*

*How can you be on her side?* I think all this, but I do not say it.

Katrina steps toward me, a little too close for comfort. "Listen, Skye. I don't know exactly what went on between you two, but Cat Island is a community of respect," she says.

If I were stronger, like if I were Zoë or Pearl, I would outright laugh at Katrina's lecture. *Respect!* I think. *What a joke.* But I'm not Pearl and I'm not Zoë, and the fact is, Katrina scares me. It's no wonder she and Amanda get along.

Katrina stops talking, takes another swig from her water bottle, and flips her hair back in this really annoying way. Apparently she's not done. "Honesty and cooperation are at the core of this experience," she says. She reaches out and rests her hand on my shoulder. When I feel her hand, I shudder.

*Yuck,* I think. *Get your hand off me.* But she doesn't move. She just looks me straight in the eyes. "You need to work things out with her, Skye," she says.

*Me? Work things out with her?*

I am so blown away, so in shock at Katrina's little lecture, that I am completely and utterly flabbergasted. For one of the few times in my life, words escape me. Not to mention that it is totally useless to argue with Katrina; it's obvious whose side she's on, and that she didn't hear the entire story. I don't want to stick around for more of this little speech.

Katrina's hand is still on my shoulder. "Listen, Skye. Can you please make an effort to communicate more effectively with Amanda?" she asks.

"Ah, yeah. Whatever," I say.

But then I say it. I have to. It's as if Pearl suddenly takes over my brain and this blast of strength just comes out. "Just so you know, I didn't do anything to provoke her, Katrina," I say. "I don't really know why she's so mad in the first—"

"Stop," she interrupts, putting up her hand like a crossing guard who's stopping traffic.

"I don't want to hear it, Skye. I just want this nonsense to end." And then Katrina fastens her helmet, straddles her bike, and pedals away.

# Sweet

"What was that all about—between you and our favorite counselor?" Mason asks me at lunch, nodding toward Katrina. "I tried to catch up to you, but by the time I pedaled all the way to the top of the hill, you were gone."

I just stand there. I am hot and dizzy, and I'm still reeling from my run-in with Katrina. Even though I had a burst of strength in the end, I still feel awful. I look back at Mason, and I don't know what to say. To tell you the truth, I'm thinking that if I actually attempt to answer him, I might lose it completely. I can feel my lip quivering, and I'm afraid that if I open my mouth or blink my eyes, that's it—I may as well just throw in the towel, get in the van, and beg Moondog to let me go home.

Mason waves his hand in front of me, trying to get my attention. "Hey, Skye, you OK?" he asks.

I look back at him and try to nod and smile, but I know if I speak, the dam will break.

"Listen," he says. "I know these last few days have been tough and all, but hang in there. Slow and steady wins the race." Mason smiles at me and squeezes my shoulder. He is so close that I can see the tiny specks of blue around his pupils, and if I don't keep my feet on the ground, I might completely float away.

# More

I wish I really *could* float away. We have finished the ride for the day, and we are sitting on the grass in a big circle: my group on one side, and Brad, Katrina, and their team on the other. I am next to Pearl, who is next to Zoë. I'm starting to get really sick of thinking about this whole Amanda thing. It's taking up way too much space in my brain. Plus, after lunch, something in me switched from sad to mad, and I'm not feeling sorry for myself anymore. I'm sick of walking on eggshells around Amanda. The more I think about it, the more I realize that Zoë's right—Amanda's the one with the problem, not me. Why should I have to change who *I* am just to make *her* feel better?

We have been instructed by Moondog to sit in a circle on the grass, next to our campsite. This is the first time that all seventeen of us have assembled together since after breakfast, when we joined hands and sang the Cat Island song and got our route directions. Everyone is looking around, waiting to see what this big, unexpected meeting is all about.

Moondog finally breaks the silence. "Welcome to The King's court!" he chuckles. He scratches his white beard and looks out at us. I sit patiently, hoping we can get this little meeting over with as soon as humanly possible. I want to go soak my bones in the hot spring that T.J. told us is up in the mountains behind our tents. Moondog continues. "It has been called to my attention that some campers feel some people are getting preferential treatment and that not everyone is pitching in and doing work evenly."

*Huh? What is he talking about?* Zoë and Pearl look over at me, equally confused. I look to T.J. and Tasha, but they just shrug their shoulders like they don't really know what he's talking about either. That's about the time it hits me.

It's so obvious. I should know by now because my stomach is churning and my internal body alarm is going off full blast.

Amanda.

Pearl, Zoë, and I all think of it at the exact same time. "Preferential treatment, my butt!" mutters Pearl, jabbing me in the side with her elbow.

Zoë turns to me. "I can't believe this! Do we really have to sit here and listen to this?" she asks.

Moondog's still talking. "Look, I know you are all tired, exhausted even. I think this would be a great chance to get a handle on how everyone's feeling. We all need to be accountable for each other and our needs." Moondog leans back, reaches into the front pocket of his shirt, and takes out a rock. It's small, round, and flat like a pancake. "I found this rock down by the bay," he says. Everyone leans in to take a closer look. "In The King's court, when you have the rock, you have the floor. It's your turn to talk." He holds the rock up over his head. "But you may not speak if you don't have the rock. Got it?"

Everyone watches as Moondog passes the rock to his right. "Caitlin," he says, "I pass you the rock. Please tell us anything you'd like to share about how you're feeling thus far on our journey." Moondog places the rock in Caitlin's hand. Caitlin is short and sweet, with strawberry-blond hair and freckles, and I feel instantly sorry for her that's she's in the other group when obviously she'd be happier with us. Everyone waits.

Caitlin coughs. "Um . . ." she says softly. She looks down at the rock, too shy to look up. She takes a deep breath and finally speaks. "I guess I'm OK. I mean, I guess—besides the fact that my butt is really sore, and my legs feel like they are going to fall off, and I'm sunburned— well, besides that," she smiles and shrugs her shoulders, "I'm fine." Everyone laughs. It's funny. Plus I think everyone, including me, is relieved that they are not the only ones with sore and tired bodies. After Caitlin breaks the ice, a dozen hands shoot up. Everyone wants the rock. It seems that everyone has something to say.

Moondog looks at Caitlin. "OK," he tells her, "toss the rock to anyone else." Caitlin extends her arm and tosses the rock across the circle. We watch as it arcs through the air and lands perfectly in Pearl's outstretched hands.

Pearl isn't shy at all. "I'm feeling pretty good. Who wouldn't be? It's so beautiful here!" she says, waving her hands toward the backdrop of mountains and the purplish-orange sunset unfolding behind us. "I just think we should all lighten up, because this is *camp,* and this is supposed to be *fun*." She looks across the circle right at Amanda. "Maybe if you all had my perspective, you would just be thankful for what you have."

# Two Hours Later

After a forty-five-minute hike up the mountain behind our tents, we find the hot spring. T.J. kneels down by the edge of the water and sticks in his hand. "The temperature is perfect!" he shouts. "I'm jumping in!"

I stand and stare at the sight three feet away from me: a perfectly round pool of crystal-clear water surrounded by smooth, flat stones and a carpet of soft, mossy grass. It's like our own private Jacuzzi—God's Jacuzzi—tucked away on Cat Island.

Mason, Charlie, and Zoë follow T.J.'s lead and jump right in with all their clothes on. Two weeks ago I probably would have stalled for courage and watched from the grass while everyone frolicked in the water. But before I know it, I'm flying through midair in my mud-stained T-shirt, leaving the old me behind and not looking back.

# Moonlight

By the time we hike back down the mountain, it's dark. With the help of the moon and my headlamp, I drag my pack out of the van and lug my stuff over to the girls' tent, where Pearl and Zoë have already set up for the evening. I change out of my wet clothes, slip into my silky pink pajamas, and hang my soaked uniform out on the clothesline. I unpack my sleeping bag and lay it down on the hard ground beside Pearl's stuff. I am extra careful to be nowhere near *you know who*'s red-and-blue plaid sleeping bag, which is sitting in a big heap across the way.

I'm almost out of the tent when I hear voices. I peek through a crack in the tent wall and see Ian, Merritt, and Amanda lying flat on their backs and staring up at the sky, talking.

"This blows!" says Ian. "If I have to listen to that dumb Cat Island song one more time, I'm going to barf."

Amanda laughs. "Yeah, or listen to Skye being such a kiss-up," she says. "Puh-leeeeeese! That girl wakes up in a good mood and it makes me sick." Amanda sticks her finger in her mouth like she's going to gag and rolls her eyes dramatically.

A sharp ripple of panic swells through my body. I know I've sworn off Amanda's spirit-breaking tirades, but for some sick reason I stay right there, peering through the tiny hole in the tent, hypnotized by the cruel conversation.

Ian snickers to himself. "I can't get out of here soon enough," he moans. Merritt isn't saying much. She is just staring up at the sky. Finally Amanda breaks the silence.

"I cannot *wait* until we get to leave this hole of an island," she says, exhaling loudly.

"I know," says Ian.

And then something weird happens. Merritt gets up.

"You guys need to lighten up a little. I mean, my parents made me come here, too, but it's not *that* bad, and I'm actually starting to kind of like it," she says, still standing. "And Skye really isn't so bad. I don't know why you are always picking on her."

I almost fall over.

*Is that really Merritt? Is she being . . . nice?* But a long squint through the small opening in the tent wall confirms my suspicions.

Merritt, it seems, has a heart.

# Make a Wish

I stand in the back of the tent and eavesdrop on Amanda, Ian, and Merritt for a few more minutes, until I really can't take it anymore. I feel kind of gross just listening to them, like their negativity might rub off on me. So I slip out of the tent and slide in next to Zoë at the campfire. Almost everyone's there, singing loudly. I move my mouth like I'm singing, too, but really I'm panning around the perimeter of the campsite looking for a certain someone.

I spot him sitting with his back up against an oak tree, writing in his journal. His curly dark hair sticks out from under his baseball cap, the broken-in brim pulled down over his eyes. He writes swiftly, like he has so much to say and not enough time. I wish I could be a little bird on his shoulder and read what he is writing. I wonder if he writes anything about me.

I look away before he catches me staring. I tilt my head back and look up at the stars. There are millions of them—millions! I've never seen anything like it. It's like somebody turned the lights on for the entire universe. It's amazing. I think about our ride today, and the hot-spring Jacuzzi, and how good and strong and whole I feel—like I might actually make it. And that very second, I see a shooting star scorching across the sky. I squint to make sure I'm seeing what I think I'm seeing, and before it's too late, I close my eyes tight and wish hard and long. I wish that I will actually make it around this island in one piece, I wish that a certain boy will like me back, and I wish for my necklace to find its way home.

# Morning

Both teams are together in a big circle, holding hands as we do every morning.

"New experiences are integral to sharpening our minds, refueling our tanks, and opening our eyes to the wonders of our potential," Moondog preaches.

Everyone is already linked together, hand in hand—everyone but me. I was rushing to get my bike tires pumped and water bottles filled, so I'm late. I glance around the circle, searching for a spot where I can slip in unnoticed. My eyes stop on the only space where the circle is broken. It's smack between . . .

Mason and Amanda.

Amanda turns, rolls her eyes like I'm the last person on earth she would like to see, and grudgingly accepts my hand. Amanda is not exactly high on my list of people I want to hold hands with. As soon as her sweaty palm touches mine, my body tenses up. To my right, Mason's fingers lace loosely around mine. It feels weird, but good-weird.

Moondog's still talking. "Today the terrain will be steep and challenging." He takes a sip of coffee from his mug. "This is probably the hardest topography we'll face on the island."

*Great*, I think, wondering if I'll make it

through the day. And then it happens.

Mason squeezes my hand—*squeezes my hand*—and a jolt shoots right up my arm from my fingertips.

I try not to smile. I try to stay calm and cool, like this kind of thing happens to me all the time. I try this, but my body has other ideas. A zillion tiny goose bumps appear all the way down my tan arms, even the arm that's attached to Amanda.

I strain to follow my brain's instructions and turn off the strange sensations that are looping through me like a bolt of electricity. I look at Moondog, who is still explaining today's route.

"Today I will be following close behind in the van. It's already seventy-five degrees and it's only seven A.M. I think we are in for an unusually hot day." He wipes his forehead with his old red bandanna. "Cougar Pass has a lot of uphills, so take it slow. Be smart out there."

Amanda's hand is sweaty, and it squirms in my hand.

"Come. *On.* People," she mutters. "How long do we have to stand here?"

"OK, that's it!" says Moondog.

"Drink lots of water," shouts Brad.

"Stay hydrated!" chirps Katrina.

"Keep pedaling," adds T.J.

"Go for it!" cheers Tasha.

# Last

I'm last—dead last. I'm behind Pearl. I'm
behind Zoë. I'm behind, well, everyone, and
I'm starting to get used to it. A few weeks ago I
would have cared, but now I just want to *survive.*
I have tried everything to distract my brain from
quitting. I have sung every song from *The Sound
of Music.* I have recited the Pledge of Allegiance
seven times. I have had entire conversations with
myself, out loud. I might be going bonkers.
I pull over to the side of the road and shout up
to the others, "I'm stopping here. You guys keep
going!" I sprawl out next to my bike.

There's no reply. I prop myself up and stare
down the path. I don't know who I thought I was
talking to, because nobody is there—not Zoë,
not Mason, not Charlie, not even Pearl, who
usually rides back with me.

*Great. Just great. They probably don't even
realize I've stopped!* I lie on the side of the road,
too tired to move, until I start to think about
rattlesnakes and the giant black flies I feel
buzzing around my head. Sweat drips off my
forehead. My hair is soaked. I close my eyes and
try to breathe.

I sit up, grab my water bottle off my bike,
and douse my sweltering face with water. I lie
back again, close my eyes, and listen to the

insects, the birds, and the pavement sizzling beneath me. And then, somehow—and I don't really know how—I scrape myself off the ground and try again.

# One Hour Later

I've been on my bike about an hour when my mind starts playing tricks on me. The path is blurry. I think I might be hallucinating. I reach down and grab my water bottle, lift it over my head, and squeeze. Water drips through the holes of my helmet, onto my hair, and down the nape of my neck. I keep pedaling. A clash of voices whispers inside my head:

*"Just take the van!"*

*"You're never going to make it."*

*"No! Don't quit now!"*

It's hot. Sweat is trickling off my nose. For entertainment, I stick my tongue out and catch the perspiration as it drips. I hear T.J. ride up behind me.

"Hey, how ya doin'?" he asks.

"Not so good," I answer weakly.

"Drink some water, Skye. Water is *so* key," he adds.

I balance myself with one hand on my handlebars and grab my water bottle with the other. Thankfully, the endless hill I've been pedaling up is more gradual now, and I can actually talk and pedal at the same time.

"Do you want me to call back to Moondog and have the van come get you?" T.J. asks.

The van. Trumpets and fireworks go off in

my head. *The van!* I picture myself sprawled out in the backseat with a cold bottle of Gatorade. But I don't want to ride into camp in the van.

"No. I'm OK," I say.

T.J. pedals up so he's right alongside me. He's so close, I could reach out and touch him. He pedals effortlessly, like he's not the slightest bit hot or tired.

"Would you like to know T.J. Malone's secret to hill climbing?" he asks.

I nod feebly. Anything would help me right about now.

"OK, first of all, picture a place you really love."

I pick up my water bottle again and squirt water all over my face. Half of it falls onto my shirt. It feels good. I keep pedaling. I drink more water. I picture this park in Ithaca my mom always takes us to.

"Do you have a place you're thinking of?" asks T.J.

"Yeah," I say. "There's this place my mom takes us. You have to hike, like, a zillion stairs to get to it, but at the very top there's this waterfall. It's like . . ." I pause, remembering the last time I was there swimming with my mom, my sisters, and Isabel. "It's so cool," I say, still pedaling.

"Sweet," T.J. says, smiling.

I'm grinning, too, because, for some reason, this is kind of fun. I'm actually sort of forgetting about the fact that we have been pedaling uphill for eight billion miles.

"OK, so here's the secret," he says. "When my legs hurt and I think I can't go any farther, I just pretend I'm at my favorite spot. For me, the place I picture is back home in North Carolina, riding my bike on our farm, looking at the cows and the dark green pastures. It works every time."

I'll try anything at this point. I pedal and picture myself hiking to the waterfall with my sisters and Isabel. T.J. interrupts my vision.

"Hey, Skye. You know, if you quit hiking up all those stairs, you'd never get to see the waterfall."

*Huh?* I think.

T.J. pedals ahead of me. He turns and shouts back, "When the going gets tough, the tough get going!" In one quick burst he takes off up the mountain.

I pedal after him. And when I look back to see where the van is, I notice something totally crazy—something I never even knew happened, something I can't believe.

I have reached the top of the mountain.

# Glacier Bay

After we clean off our bikes, bathe, eat, wash the dishes, and put up the tents, Tasha appears. She's holding a large stuffed sack with the word *Mail* printed in bold black letters down the side.

"Hey," Tasha calls. "Moondog picked this up with the food run yesterday." She drags the sack over by the campfire. After the ride today, this surprise could not have come at a better time.

We descend on Tasha and the mailbag like flies on honey. Everyone gets something, including me.

Hey, Skye!
What's up, Super Girl? ☺ How's your butt feeling from all that biking? The neighborhood is not the same without you! I hope you are having fun. I've been running every morning to the high school and back. For soccer we have to be able to run two miles in under 14 minutes, or we don't even get to try out. No problem! I have so much more to tell you. I miss you!!

Come home already!!!

Love always,

Isabel

Ms. Skye O'Shea
Cat Island Adventure Camp
P.O. Box 33
Cat Island, B.C.
V0R 2K0
Canada

Dear Skye,

Sweetheart, how are you? We have all been thinking about you lots, and sending you tons of love! I spoke with your counselor, Tasha, and she says you got there safe and sound and that you are doing marvelously. I know it's hard to be so far away, but you are going to feel great when you get through this. What an accomplishment! You will be the only one in our family who has ever biked around an island!

How do you like the Pacific Ocean? The stars at night must be spectacular! Well, darling, we can't wait to hear every detail. I love you to pieces, and I am thinking about you often. Your sisters are doing great and they say hi — Dad does too! We all send you hugs and kisses!

xxxx 0000!

Love,
Mom

# Three Days Later

Mason is acting weird. Really weird. He's not really talking to any of us, especially me. He's being kind of mean—well, not mean, but distant. He didn't want to swim after riding today, and he didn't want to roast marshmallows with us. When I smiled at him by the campfire, he just looked away.

I have decided it's me. Obviously he can sense that I like him, and obviously he must not like me back, and he doesn't know how to break it to me. Every time I think about it, a wave of gloom washes over me.

So when Tasha tells us we have an hour of quiet time before we have to turn in for the night, I decide to be the brave new me and talk to him. I have nothing to lose. I don't know where this new power comes from, but it feels good to deal with things instead of just obsessively worrying about them, like I used to do with Amanda. I make my way through the woods and down the hill through the high grass. I find Mason sitting on a rock at the base of Half-Moon Bay. For a few seconds I hide behind a fir tree, resting my back against the trunk. I seriously consider wimping out, because, let's face it, when it comes to boys, I'm completely clueless. But somehow my feet carry me toward

him. Mason hears me approaching and looks up,
but he doesn't wave or smile.

*Great. He hates me.*

*Retreat.*

*Get away now, while you still can,* I think.

But the weird thing is, even though my
heart's beating kind of fast, I am calm and cool,
and there is not a single alarm going off in my
body. I take a big, deep breath and sit down on a
rock beside him. The night is warm and clear,
and the moon is glowing over the water.

"Hey," I say. (Original, I know, but it's the
best I can do.) While I wait for him to answer
me, I look at him and decide that no matter
what, there's no denying it—he is so cute, so
nice, so not like all the other boys at this camp.
And what drives me most crazy is that, for some
strange reason, ever since Mason started being
unfriendly, I started liking him even more.

About ten zillion uncomfortable minutes
later, Mason finally speaks. "Hey," he says, his
eyes now glued to the ground.

I try desperately to think of something smart
and cute and funny to say. "How's it going?" is all
that comes out.

*Cool, Skye. Real cool.*

No response. Mason just sits there, like I'm
not even sitting next to him, like I'm a ghost.

I look out at the water and hope that he says something soon.

"I'm *all right*," he finally says softly.

I don't say anything. Let's face it, he does not seem *all right*. I don't say that, though; I just think it. I sit there and wait and stare up at the stars. I do not look at him. I do not say anything.

I gulp, preparing to tell him that he doesn't have to like me back, that he shouldn't worry about it, that we can just go back to being normal friends. "Umm," I start. "Well . . ."

Mason lifts his head and looks at me. "I've got to tell you something," he interrupts. When he turns his face into the moonlight, I notice he's been crying.

I just kind of stare at him. I don't know what to say. But before I have to think of anything, he speaks. "Someone stole my journal," he says. "They took it two nights ago while I was sleeping. I can't find it anywhere."

*What?* "Your journal?" I ask. *Why would anyone want to steal his journal?*

Mason turns away from me and stares out at the water while he talks. "At first, I thought I might have misplaced it or whatever, but I never lose track of it. I always put it in a special side pocket of my backpack, but when I went to write in it, it was gone."

Right at this moment, Mason looks so incredibly sad that I just want to reach out and tell him everything is going to be OK. But at the same time, this other side of me is overwhelmed with relief. *He's not mad at me! He still likes me!* I think selfishly. I take my head out of the clouds and plant my feet back on the ground.

"Oh, wow," I say. "That's terrible."

Mason picks up a rock and heaves it sidearm into Half-Moon Bay. We both watch silently as it skips a dozen times over the waves.

"Why do people have to be such jerks?" he asks.

I pick up a rock and sling it out into the water. "Maybe we should tell T.J. or Tasha, so they could, you know, help you find it," I say.

Mason picks up another stone and throws it with all his might. "I know who did it. She left me this note." He reaches into his pocket and pulls out a crunched-up piece of paper. "Here," he says, handing it to me. I unfold the paper and hold it up to the moonlight. I can barely make out the handwriting.

Mason,

Your life is very interesting. Juicy! Deep! Thanks for sharing.

If you want this thing back, follow these steps:

1. Don't tell anyone.
2. Stop being such a Goody Two-Shoes!

As soon as I read it my body alarm goes off, and lately my alarm has been reserved for one certain person on this island. It's obvious. Amanda. *Who else would pull off something as mean and stupid and pointless as this?*

"We've got to tell T.J.," I say.

Mason shakes his head. "No. Thanks for caring and everything, but I'm going to take care of this my own way." And then, for the first time in the last forty-eight hours, Mason looks up at me and smiles.

# Nineteen Minutes Later

Back at my tent, I'm steaming mad. Even though everyone is already asleep, I rifle through my day pack until I find my tiny feather and lucky stone. I grab Tasha's red pocketknife that's lying out on top of her bag and cut eight inches off the thin bungee cord on the side of my pack. I return Tasha's knife and move out of the tent into the moonlight. I carefully thread the cord around the stem of the feather and through the hole in my lucky stone. I reach up and pull it around my neck, tying the cord tight in back. I'm ready. I'm armed. Somebody might want to warn Amanda.

# Two Days Later

We're all eating breakfast. Moondog is pouring the last bit of pancake batter onto the griddle when he makes a loud announcement. "Cat Island is about kinship, teamwork, and cooperation!" he booms. "Today we're going to change things a little—mix it up, so to speak. Everyone will be paired with someone from the opposite group." Everybody shuffles and moans, wary of The King's experiment. "It's just for one day," he promises.

A loud rumbling noise comes from the dirt road, and in unison everybody turns and looks. It's T.J.

He's driving up in the camp van, pulling a huge metal trailer stacked with brightly colored sea kayaks. Everyone lets out a round of "oohs" and "ahhs," like they're watching fireworks on the Fourth of July.

Moondog smiles, his big surprise unveiled. "As you can see, we are going to be doing something a little different today." He walks to the sea kayaks and knocks on the siding. "This, my friends, will be a little challenge in teamwork. As I'm sure you know from studying your route maps, we are at Catalina Point, but we need to get to Tyson's Point."

I jump up, walk over to my bike, and slip my

route map out of the carrying case attached to my handlebars. Everybody else does the same thing. I settle back down, following along with my map as Moondog talks.

"To get back on the trail, we either need to follow it all the way around White Tooth Bay, or we can cross the bay right here." Moondog points to the map. "Kayaking across the bay is the fastest route, unless, of course, you want to drive all the way around." Moondog laughs. "But driving in a stuffy old van wouldn't be an adventure, now would it?"

*This is going to be fun,* I think, crossing every finger and hoping I get a good partner like Caitlin or Becca and just not *you know who*. Pearl leans over and whispers in my ear. "No biking for an entire day? Sounds good to me!"

I nod in agreement. Zoë turns to both of us. "Oh my gosh. I've always wanted to kayak. How fun is this?"

Moondog's still talking. "This is going to be hard-core paddling. We'll be traveling on a pretty swift current in these kayaks built for two. They are seaworthy and hard to tip, but be careful!" Everybody is excited and alert, sitting up straight. Even Katrina's group is paying attention. "The bay is breathtakingly beautiful, and if we're lucky, we might see some orca from a distance." Moondog walks toward the van. "I'm going to pack up and meet you with the van at Tyson's Point. Who's ready for some paddling?" he shouts.

"Woo-hooo! Let's do it!" hollers T.J.

I join the swarm of campers in front of Moondog to hear my fate.

# Just My Luck

Of course, you guessed it. As soon as I heard about the teamwork thing, I knew it would happen, too. I was sure of it. So when Moondog calls out, "Merritt, you're with Skye," I just accept it. At least I'm not with Amanda. And maybe my batteries are running low, but my body alarm doesn't even go off. Everyone takes turns helping to carry the colorful sea kayaks to the shore. It's exciting and different, and I am relieved to have a day off my bike.

Merritt walks over to me. "You want to get the paddles?" she asks, perfectly nicely. "I'll get the life jackets and meet you down by the water."

"OK," I say, heading for the back of the van. I fish my cowgirl hat out from my pack, smear white goopy sunscreen all over my already sunburned face, and grab two long wooden paddles.

After T.J. gives us instructions on steering and safety, we're ready to go. Amanda and Zack take off first, right alongside Tasha and Katrina.

"Have fun!" I shout, hoping Amanda doesn't eat poor Zack alive.

T.J. walks over to the rocky shore and cups his hands up to his mouth. "Paddle hard, pal!" he shouts to Zack, who waves back at him.

Everybody else lines up to push off.
Mason and Peter.
Pearl and Caitlin.
Becca and Zoë.
Charlie and Ian.
Merritt and me.
T.J. and Brad.

# Paddle

Merritt is in the front of our bright yellow sea kayak. I sit in the back, which means I control the foot pedals attached to the rudder that steers the kayak. T.J. is right; it's easy. We paddle for the first few minutes in awkward silence, until Merritt finally breaks the ice.

"So where'd you get that cowgirl hat, anyway?" she asks. "I love that thing." Merritt's friendliness takes me a little by surprise. I have my guard up. Even though I heard her that night in the tent, she's still friends with the meanest person I've ever met in my life. I stare at the back of her orange life jacket, watch her platinum-blond ponytail bobbing back and forth, and keep paddling.

"Well," I start to answer.

Merritt interrupts. "So, like, did you bring it from home, or did you get it on a trip?"

I struggle to paddle, steer, and talk at the same time. "Umm, one of my best friends gave it to me for good luck. You know, for the trip."

"Cool."

More awkward silence. We paddle, working into a rhythm. One stroke on the right. One stroke on the left. One stroke on the right. One stroke on the left. I look up at the seagulls soaring above us, and around me at the mountains and canyons on either side. It's beautiful and still. We are paddling with the current, dancing on the water.

Merritt turns and smiles back at me. "So, how'd you hook up with that hottie Mason?"

*Oh boy.*

*Where did that come from?*

*I didn't know my crush was so obvious.*

"Oh, ahh . . . we're just friends," I say, blushing. For one thing, it's true. I mean, we haven't, like, kissed or anything. We just like each other. Besides, I'm not crazy! I'm not going to talk about Mason with *Merritt!*

Merritt grins. "Oh, I *seeeee*," she says. "Just friends, huh?"

But the thing is, she's not being mean. She's joking and funny and saying everything in a friendly kind of way. She's actually being nice.

We paddle more. One stroke on the right. One stroke on the left. One stroke on the right. One stroke on the left.

As we round the bend I struggle to steer us along the curve of the bay. Merritt turns around again. "Hey, what's up with this boating stuff?" she says. "Did you notice this in the catalog?" She laughs.

"It's kind of fun," I say back. "Don't you think?"

She flips her paddle in the water, splashing me with the tip of the oar. *"Real fun!"* she giggles, showering me with cool water.

And I think we are starting to be friends.

# Four Hours Later

My nose is burning, my skin is peeling, and my arms feel like they are going to fall right off, but Tyson's Point is finally within view. We paddle and paddle. Merritt is strong. With her powerful strokes thrusting the boat forward, we surf along the water at a fast pace. I don't know if it's the rhythmic trance of paddling or what, but I decide to ask her the big question I've wanted to ask ever since it felt safe, ever since it felt like she wouldn't go running to Amanda and tell her everything we talked about.

"Hey, can I ask you a question?" I say between strokes.

"Sure, shoot," she says.

"OK, well, I was wondering . . ." I stop short of finishing my sentence. *Is this a good idea?* But my body alarm is not ringing or even buzzing, so I continue. I look at Merritt's ponytail swinging back and forth in front of me, and I just say it. "What's up with Amanda? Why does she hate me so much?" As soon as it leaves my mouth I feel relieved, like it's out of my head, out of my mind, out of my body.

"Oh, she doesn't *hate* you," answers Merritt. "Trust me, it's not you, Skye."

*Uh, can you elaborate on that?* I think, but I don't say that. I just paddle and wait.

"Trust me, it is definitely not you," she says again.

"But my necklace," I start, "and she always glares at me, like she—"

Merritt stops me before I can go on. "I know, she told me about the necklace." She lifts her paddle out of the water and rests it on top of her lap. I do the same thing, and for a second, neither of us says a word. We just float, the current carrying us.

We glide in silence until Merritt grasps both sides of the kayak and turns back to look at me. She looks very serious, like she's about to tell me something that's hard to say. She takes a deep breath. "OK, Skye. Nobody really knows what I'm about to tell you except the counselors and Moondog." She steadies herself, her hands gripping both sides of the kayak. My stomach churns like it does when I know someone's about to tell me something really bad. Merritt looks at me from across the kayak and speaks slowly. "Amanda's mom died a few weeks before she came here."

*Huh?*

*What?*

My stomach does that dropping thing right down to the very pit, and even though Amanda has been mean to me, I feel terrible—terrible and sad. I can't even think of anything to say. I pick up my paddle and dig into the water, but it's useless. Without Merritt's help, we hardly move.

Merritt is still facing me, her paddle resting across her lap. "Listen, Skye. She's been really awful to you, and just because her mom died—I mean it's totally sad and everything—but that doesn't mean she can go around being nasty to anyone she feels like picking on."

My brain is still back at Amanda's mom. I am wondering how she died and why she died. *Was she sick? Was it a car accident? Was it sudden?* I think. A rush of panic about my own mom floods my brain and I suddenly miss her very much.

Merritt turns away from me and starts paddling again. She keeps talking. "Amanda just has a lot of problems, and she's taking them out on you. You're an easy target because, well, people just like you. They like being around you. You're fun. I guess for Amanda, you're an easy target because she's so *miserable.*"

We paddle some more. "But you know," Merritt starts again, "it's definitely not cool the way she's treated you. Really, there's no excuse."

Merritt sighs, like she's worn out, and then starts talking again. "I mean, even I feel bad that I haven't really stood up to her. Someone really needs to tell her she can't go around doing stuff like that. There are other ways to work things out when you're depressed."

*Whoa.* I don't know what to say. Merritt is being really nice and cool, and I'm feeling terrible for all the things I've thought about her this entire trip. Merritt turns back, still paddling, and looks at me.

"Listen," she says. "For the rest of the trip, I have some advice for you. Steer clear of her. because Amanda is just really sad she'd never admit that to anyone.

I nod, and that's it. Merritt turns around.

We paddle and glide, paddle and glide, paddle and glide along the water. We are fast and strong and smooth. We are in sync.

"Skye?" Merritt says, breaking the silence. "You're pretty cool there, Super Girl."

"Thanks," I say. "You, too."

And I mean it.

*Ithaca: flowers*
*® 1999 J. Paul*

Dear Mom an
How are you?
awesome tim
hard at first,
it, and I'm r
still hard, b
have two frie
Pearl only ha
SO cool! Ho
Shannon? T
love them c
home soon

*he wildlife garden.*

ad,
having an
Camp was really
now I'm used to
homesick. It's
t's really fun. I
s, Zoë and Pearl.
e leg and she's
re Shel and
everyone that I
that I will be
miss you!!!

P.P.S. I love you!!!

WETLAND

HABITATS

Mom + Dad
The O'Shea Family
Fairway Drive
Ithaca, NY 14850

Love, Yours Truly,
Skye O'Shea #17

P.S. I can't wait to take a bath as soon as I get home!!!

# Pelican Bay

Ever since our sea-kayak extravaganza, all seventeen of us have taken to biking in one big group. I usually hang out in the back with Pearl and Zoë and sometimes Peter and Mason. But we all ride together, and we eat lunch together, and we don't group apart like we used to. The biggest change isn't really Amanda. She's still shooting me dirty looks, rolling her eyes, and whispering behind my back to Ian. No, the biggest change is actually *me*. I'm flat-out not scared of Amanda anymore. It's like she's been declawed, her venom extracted. I actually find myself feeling sorry for her. I mean, don't get me wrong. I don't want to *hang out* with her. Let's not get carried away. But ever since I found out Amanda's secret, she doesn't make me tremble.

# Shhh

It's one A.M. I shake Pearl and Zoë until they both wake up. "It's time," I whisper. The three of us slither out of our sleeping bags, just as we'd planned, and tiptoe out of the tent. We sneak across the big grassy field to the van.

"Do you have your headlamp?" whispers Pearl.

"Headlamp," I say, switching it on. We are pretending to be secret agents, but we're doing more giggling than anything else. I open the back of the van and shine the headlamp onto the pile of gear and luggage crammed inside. Zoë starts digging through the mound of bags. "Where does she usually keep it?" she asks.

Pearl starts flipping through the pile, too. "What color is it?" she quizzes me.

"It's green," I whisper, "lime green." My heart flutters and, for a split second, I wonder if we should be doing this. I mean, this isn't my stuff, and— "Ahh, you guys, maybe we should just leave it," I say.

"No way, Skye!" say Zoë and Pearl in unison.

"Just chill. It's OK," says Pearl, still searching for the bag.

Zoë suddenly stops and starts jumping up and down, holding her right foot. "Ouch! You stepped on my toe!" she says.

"Hey, it's not like I have any feeling down there." Pearl giggles.

"Shhh, you guys. We gotta keep it down," I remind them. But it's hard not to laugh.

Zoë digs her hand down deep into the maze of bags. "Found it!" she whispers, hauling out the enormous green gear bag and dragging it over to the willow tree farthest away from the campsite.

The three of us quietly go to work. First I unzip the bag and poke my hand around until I find what I'm looking for: a small purple bag at the bottom of the heap of black clothes. "Got it," I say, holding it up for my co-conspirators to see. Pearl shines the light onto the bag, and we all peer in as I carefully unzip it.

"Jackpot!" I whisper, pulling out Mason's small leather-bound journal.

Pearl pats me on the back. "Nice work, ace."

Zoë shines the light on the side pocket of the lime green bag. "Hey, we're not done yet," she says. She carefully unzips the side pocket and reaches in, feeling around inside.

"Do you feel it?" I ask.

"Not yet," she says. I take the light from Zoë and hold it steady.

"She told me it's there. It has to be," I say.

Zoë smiles. "What do we have here?" She

pulls her hand out of the bag and dangles my lucky necklace in front of my eyes, swinging the arrowhead back and forth like she's trying to hypnotize me.

"Nice!" I say, happy to have my luck back.

Pearl stands behind me. "May I please do the honors?" she says, untying my homemade stone/feather/cord necklace and dropping it into my hand. Pearl pushes my ponytail away from my neck and strings the lucky arrowhead around me. "Home sweet home," she says, tying it tightly.

I get up off the ground and reach out my hand to help Pearl up.

"Two down, one to go," says Zoë, rubbing her hands together.


Pearl shines the light up to my face. "Do you have the stuff?" she asks.

I reach into my day pack and pull out the box. "Do you think she'll know to open it?" I ask. "I mean, do you think she can tell it's for her?"

Pearl shines the light directly onto the box, reaches out her hand, and removes the lid. "I'm just going to look one more time," she says.

Zoë puts her finger up to her lips. "Shhh," she whispers. We all stare at the smooth, light-green piece of sea glass we found on the rocky ocean shore. When I take the leather cord out of the box, the glass glitters in the light from the headlamp. "How'd you get the cord around it, Skye?" Zoë asks.

"It had a little hole at the top. See?" I say, pointing to the tiny hole. "I just wove it right through."

"Nice work, ace," says Pearl, patting the top of my head. We hear a noise. It's only the wind blowing, but it jolts us back into high gear. I gently drop the necklace back into the box, reach into my pocket for the note, and hand it to Zoë. She reads it out loud one last time.

Amanda,

   We were really, really
sorry to hear about your mom.
We can't imagine how it must
feel to lose someone so
special. We hope you like
this necklace we made you.
It's made of sea glass,
which gets more dazzling the
longer it is knocked around
at sea. You are very strong
to come to camp after
such a sad thing happened.
We admire your courage,
and we're sorry—
   really, truly sorry.
Love,
       Zoë    Pearl    Skye

Zoë looks up. "Sound good?" she asks. She carefully folds up the note and hands it back to me. I tuck it into the box with the necklace, place it into the same purple bag Mason's journal was in, and wedge the bag back into Amanda's lime green duffel.

Pearl and Zoë straddle the bag and push the sides together. I pull the zipper until we seal the bag up, just as we found it. Zoë hoists the entire bag over her shoulder, carries it back to the van, and plops it onto the heap of gear bags. The three of us creep back to our tent without a sound.

# Four Hours Later

I wake up before anyone is stirring and slip
out of my sleeping bag. It's still dark. I grab my
headlamp, feel around the ground by my stuff
for Mason's journal, and tiptoe out of our tent.
The smooth leather binding burns a hole in my
hand as I slink across the grassy field to the boys'
tent a hundred yards away. Evil voices inside my
head badger me. *Open it! He'll never know.* My
body alarm is going off, and nobody else is even
around.

*Don't do it.*
*Don't do it.*
*Don't do it.*

A few feet before the boys' tent, I take a big
gasp of air. I look down at the journal and feel
the smooth cover, the tattered edges of the
paper, and—right before I do something I might
really regret—something catches my eye.

It's Mason.

He's outside.

Asleep.

He's curled up in a dark green sleeping bag
like a caterpillar stowed away in his cocoon. My
heart is pounding wildly. *What if he wakes up
and sees me and thinks I'm the one that took his
journal in the first place?* I stare, frozen, at his
back two feet away. *Breathe,* I think, feeling my

breath as I kneel down behind him. I gingerly unzip his day pack and slip the journal into the special side pocket where Mason told me he keeps it.

I look at his back rising and falling as he sleeps. *Don't move. Sleep.* I send him telepathic messages. Then I sprint all the way back to my tent, slip inside my warm sleeping bag, and drift off to sleep.

# Three Hours Later

I am sipping my hot cocoa by the morning campfire when Mason comes running up to me.

"Hey!" he says, all happy and back to his regular, normal, friendly self. He sits down next to me on the ground. My heart gets all swirly and does this weird thumping rhythm it seems to reserve for awkward romantic moments. Mason is wearing a black hooded sweatshirt with *Milton Academy Soccer* printed across the chest. He's out of breath from running. "You're never going to believe this!" he blurts out.

I return his smile, like I have no idea what he's about to tell me. "What's up?" I ask innocently.

Mason points to the pouch in his sweatshirt. "I got it back," he tells me.

I open my eyes wide, as if I'm surprised, as if I don't really know what he's talking about. "Got what back?" I ask, baiting him.

Mason leans in close. His lips practically brush up against my ear. My body alarm does not go off, not even one little bell.

"My journal!" he whispers. "I think Amanda felt guilty or something." He shrugs. "When I woke up this morning, it was right back where I always keep it. I guess her conscience must have gotten the best of her." He smiles.

I smile back at him, not sure what to say. In a rare move by me—very rare—I keep my mouth shut. The silence hovers over us. The birds are chirping. The morning clouds are clearing—blue sky and sunshine peek through. "Sorry I was in such a bad mood before," he says. His knee is now brushing against my knee. "I was just bummed, I guess."

It is at this moment that I notice his eyes are so blue, so bright, so—

Mason interrupts my daydream. "Hey, I'm gonna get ready for the ride." He stands up. "Thanks, Skye!" he says, and then he turns and runs into the breaking day.

# The Next Day

At the crack of dawn I wake up in the tent, and I'm not even tired. I do not roll out of my sleeping bag and drag myself up, my bones creaking like they have the last eighteen days before this one.

This morning I bounce. I bounce and jump and leap up. Pearl and Zoë do too, and the three of us run all the way to Snowy Owl Bay, skipping through the high grass and tumbling down the hill until we reach the rocky shore. The water is still, and it sparkles in the morning sun. Pearl sits down and unfastens her leg. "I'm jumping in!" she shouts, tearing off all her clothes except for her underwear and bra. She scrambles onto the biggest boulder and leaps in. "Come on!" she shouts from the water.

Zoë takes a quick glance around to make sure nobody from camp is approaching. She leaves her clothes in a heap and, with one running leap, dashes into the cold water. "Oooooeeee!" she screams. "Come on, Skye!"

Before I can change my mind, I toss my sweatpants and T-shirt by Zoë's pile, take a running start, and jump into the icy water. I swim underwater with my eyes wide open, like a mermaid, supported by the sea. I finally come up for air and slick my hair out of my eyes.

We splash and swim and wash our hair, and by the time we get out, the sun is all the way up. We dress quickly, giggling about our morning dip, blissful that we are almost done, almost to the end of the trail. Zoë ties her shoes, Pearl snaps her leg back on, and I sit back on the warm rocks and soak up the sun.

"Do you think she's found it yet?" I ask them, wondering about Amanda. Pearl hops up, looks over at me, and smiles. "We'll just have to wait and see," she says.

Zoë jumps up. "Let's race!" she says. The three of us sprint up the hill to breakfast.

# Mt. Tennison

Our morning meeting is later than usual. By the time we're all ready to go, it's almost time for lunch. Moondog lectures us. "Listen up," he says, sounding more serious than usual. "We have reached the final day of our ride."

We interrupt and cheer like crazy.

"Yeah!" shouts T.J.

"Wooweee!" says Zack.

Moondog waits until we simmer down before he starts up again. "Yes, indeed," he says, "this is a very special day. The view from the top of Mt. Tennison is spectacular, and the ride down will be exhilarating." He clears his throat and pauses for what seems like forever. "Our number one enemy today is complacency," he says, and then he repeats the word, slowly sounding it out. "Com-pla-cen-cy."

I look around the circle. I have no idea what this word means and, by the looks of it, neither does anybody else. Moondog gets the hint.

"What I mean is that we are all used to riding. It's easy now. It's second nature. You get on your bike, you pedal, you laugh, you talk, you ride. We've done it for three straight weeks. You are so used to it and so good at it that you could probably do it with your eyes closed." Everyone laughs. "OK, maybe not with your eyes closed."

Moondog grins. "But you don't have to think too much about what you're doing. Your body just does it for you."

I know just what Moondog's talking about, and I nod in agreement. He takes off his hat and rubs his brow. "What I want to remind you is that it's when you're the most relaxed and the least alert that accidents happen."

Dead silence.

I've been secretly thankful that no one has gotten hurt yet, and I really don't want to jinx it now. Moondog looks at us somberly and raises his voice. "What I ask each of you today is to be alert, be safe, and have fun. Enjoy the day but, above all else, use your noggin!"

# Twenty-three Miles to Go

Before I get on my bike to leave, Pearl and I wait in line to fill our water bottles from the big orange Gatorade containers. Zoë has already left with Tasha, Peter, Caitlin, and Merritt (who, ever since the day in the kayak, hasn't been glued as much to *you know who*). Pearl is busy talking to Mason and T.J. when *she* comes up to me—it's Amanda. She's wearing her custom-made Cat Island uniform and a red bandanna tied around her head.

"Hey," she says, smiling as though all of a sudden she's my best friend. I am thinking, *She found our note. She found the necklace.* But when I look closer, she doesn't have anything around her neck. I don't say anything because that's what Pearl, Zoë, and I agreed on. Zoë says good deeds are better left unsaid—something about doing them for yourself, not for thank-yous, or something like that. "It's not really a pure good deed if you're expecting something in return," she told us.

Amanda looks around nervously. "Hey, can I ride with you guys?"

*Ride with us?*

*Ride with ME?*

My gut drops right down to the ground.

And the thing that really gets me is that she's

159

acting like it's not really a big deal, like she hasn't done anything to me that would make me want to run for cover. It's like she's not even aware of her own venomous nature.

"Sure," I blurt out.

"Cool," says Amanda.

It's not like I can say no. We're the only ones left besides T.J.

I'm the last to leave the campsite. I sit on my bike and soak everything in. I'm too excited to let Amanda get in the way of my enjoying the last day. I strap my helmet on for the very last time, look ahead at Mason, Amanda, T.J., and Pearl riding a few feet up the road, and rub my necklace. Moondog's "be careful" message booms in my head. We only have twenty-three miles to go, and I don't want to blow it. I don't want to fall off and split my head open, crash into someone else at top speed, or have to listen to Amanda flip out. I rub the lucky arrowhead between my thumb and index finger.

*Please let me make it one more day.*

# Six Hours Later

I can't believe it, but out of the five of us, I'm the first to reach the top of Mt. Tennison. It's like I'm floating, or I switched legs with Wonder Woman. I'm not even tired. At the very tip of Mt. Tennison, I pull over to the side of the road. I lay my bike down on the grass, grab my water bottle, and sit on the edge of the cliff that overlooks the busy village below. The sun is bright and the sky is pure, radiant blue. There's not a cloud to be seen. I can see clear across the bay to the ocean.

From the top of Mt. Tennison the trail looks long and twisting. I can't believe I rode around an entire island! I can't believe I beat everyone up the mountain! I look around to see if anyone has joined me, but I'm still alone. I take off my helmet and place it on the grass, lie back, and stare up at the sky.

"Woo-hooo!" Pearl shouts.

"That was one big hill!" yells Mason.

I sit up and watch. First Pearl, then Mason, then Amanda, and finally T.J. reach the top of the peak.

"Yeah!" shouts T.J., setting down his bike and high-fiving me. "Go, girl!"

The five of us lie on the grass and look out at the view until T.J. reminds us that we should get going. "We don't want to be riding into town too late." He points to his watch. "There are going to be cars down there," he warns. "Remember, single file."

We climb back on our bikes and get ready for the descent back into civilization. I'm about to push off when Mason speaks. "Hey, I have an idea," he says. We all look at him. He's straddling his bike, his tan arms steadying him in place. "Let's all ride into town together." And right there, on the top of Mt. Tennison, a deal is struck. The five of us, riding in one straight row, zoom down the hill together.

# Civilization

I have never been so happy to see a toilet in my life. I have my very own. We all do. It's a big surprise when we get to the Tennison Inn, this big fancy mansion that overlooks the bay. First we have to pack our bikes away in the yellow moving truck, and then Tasha hands out the keys. With my key wedged between my front teeth, I lug my backpack, my day pack, and my body up four flights of stairs to room 403. I drop my luggage in the hallway outside my door and spit the key out into my hand. I put the key in the lock and turn the handle, pushing the door with all my weight until it swings open wide.

The room is luxurious. I take off my shoes and throw my packs down on the thick plush carpet. The sunset streams through the big bay window. A queen-size bed as big as my mom and dad's occupies the middle of the room. And that's not all. A fluffy white bathrobe with "Tennison Inn" embroidered in script on the chest pocket is laid out on top of the quilted bedspread. "Whoa!" I say out loud when I see the fancy robe. "Whoa! Whoa! Whoa!"

Even though I don't need to, I sit on the toilet anyway, just because it's there and I haven't sat on one in twenty entire days! I stand up and look around. *This is the life!* I say to myself.

I strip off every layer of my grimy, muddy, ripped-up clothing and toss each filthy piece onto the shiny tiled bathroom floor.

The bathtub is one of those old-fashioned ones with claw feet and high white sides. I turn on the water and let it run until it's just the right temperature. I sit on the edge of the tub, unwrap every little bar of soap I can find, and toss them in one by one until bubbles spill over the edge. When I slip into the tub, my body tingles and purrs. "Ahhh," I say out loud to nobody but me.

I lean back in the tub, resting my head at one end and, at the other end, sticking my feet up on the polished gold faucet. I admire my strong legs, the new muscles that have popped out right above my knees, the funny tan from where my shorts and T-shirt have been. I compare my dark, tanned arms to my pale white stomach. Then I fish around for one of the bars of soap and scrub every inch of me until I smell like roses.

"Skye. Let's go! We're late!" It's Pearl and Zoë banging on the door to my room. "Let us in!" they say in concert. I'm still in the tub, my eyes closed, a smile stuck permanently on my face. I've slipped into that in-between place where you're almost asleep but you're not. The banging and the voices snap me out of it. I rinse off the bubbles and hoist myself out.

I tiptoe from the bathroom to the bedroom, leaving a trail of drips and bubbles on the carpet. I wrap myself in the thick Tennison Inn robe, walk to the door, and peer through the little peephole just for fun, even though I know who's there.

Zoë and Pearl are standing in the hallway. "Wow!" I say, opening the door. "You guys look beautiful!" And they do. Pearl has showered and changed into a light blue dress. Her eyes are gleaming. Zoë is wearing a black miniskirt and long-sleeved pink blouse. She has tiny specks of glitter on her cheeks and her hair shines like it did the first day I met her.

I wave them into the room and throw myself down on the enormous bed. "Is this awesome or what?" I say, bouncing up and down in my extra-plush white robe.

Pearl walks over to the bay window. "Nice digs," she croons, admiring my view of Kingfisher Bay.

Zoë flops down next to me on my bed and bounces with me on the springy mattress. "You better get a move on, girl," she says, smiling. "Dinner's in five minutes!"

I grab my outfit and lock myself in the bathroom. "I'll just be a minute," I tell them. I brush my hair and, throwing caution to the wind, let it fall down around my face and neck. I slather the entire bottle of rose-scented lotion over my skin and slip into the light blue sundress my mom got me just for this occasion. I glance at my suntanned face in the mirror above the sink and smile back at my reflection.

# Dinner

When we enter the dining room, everyone is milling around the long fancy table. They look transformed. T.J. is wearing a tie and a light blue dress shirt. The other boys have on collared shirts and khakis, no jeans—even Ian. I spot Mason at the end of the table and he waves me over to the empty seat next to him. "Hey, guys, come down here," he shouts across the noisy room.

I sit between Mason and Zoë, across from Pearl and Tasha. I hardly recognize Moondog in his crisp white shirt and red bow tie, his bushy white hair neatly combed. Moondog taps a silver dinner spoon against his water glass to get everyone's attention, until the chatter dies down and all eyes are on him.

"Wow, is this the same crew I've spent the last twenty days with?" he asks jokingly. "You clean up nice! Please join me in a blessing," he says, sitting back down in his seat and reaching for Tasha's and Peter's hands on either side of him. I feel Mason's hand grab mine under the table, and I reach out and hold Zoë's hand, too. As soon as Mason touches me, I feel tingly and it's very hard to concentrate, but I try to focus on Moondog.

"I would like to thank all of you for sharing

your incredible spirits with us on this adventure," he says. "Tomorrow we head out into the world on our life's journeys. Let's celebrate this special night together." Moondog pauses. The table is silent. Mason squeezes my hand. *For real.* I get the heart thing, the woozy thing, the you-are-so-cute-I-can't-believe-you-are-holding-my-hand thing. Everything floods my head until the room is spinning. I look over at him to smile, but he's looking down, like everyone else, his eyes closed. Moondog continues. "I would love it if we could all say the final blessing together," he says. "Please join me." We lift each other's hands up high in the air like a big human chain.

"Blessings on the meal," we say together.

"Dig in!" Moondog adds.

For dinner I eat fresh salmon, salad, rice, and a side order of French fries. We all get big pieces of double-chocolate cake and vanilla ice cream for dessert. Everything melts in my mouth. After we eat, Moondog clinks his glass with the spoon again and stands up. "I have an announcement," he says, waiting for us to quiet down. "We have a special presentation to make. Let's all move into the bigger room." He points toward the entrance hall. We file out of the dining room and into the Tennison Inn lobby.

Some people lie down on the fancy oriental

carpet. Others sink into the huge cushy sofas around the fireplace. I sit on the floor, lean my back against the wall, and watch the scene unfold. The counselors move to the front, each of them holding a stack of papers and a small bag in their hands. A hush comes over the crowded room. Katrina goes first.

"Go, girl!" shouts Amanda. Katrina starts. "You all should be extremely proud of yourselves," she says. "I know I'm proud of you!" She smiles right at Amanda. I sit back and listen to her, trying not to make eye contact because, to tell you the truth, I still don't really like her. But it's the last day, so I grin and bear it.

After Katrina talks, Tasha walks up to the front of the room. "Wow," she says, smiling. "You made it!" Everyone cheers. "You pushed your comfort zones and expanded your horizons." She pauses for a few seconds, taking time to look at us all around the room. "I wish each and every one of you many, many more adventures. As my grandma used to tell me, there is never a road you can't travel, never a path you can't traverse. Always live your dreams!"

Next up is T.J. As he walks to the front of the room, Mason and Zack shout out in approval, "T.J.!" He smiles back at them, and Zoë jumps up and snaps a picture with her disposable camera.

T.J. looks strong and handsome in his blue shirt and tie, like you'd find him in Abercrombie and Fitch or J. Crew, or one of those clothes catalogs my sisters get. He clears his throat. "Y'all have majorly impressed me," he tells us. "What I'm proudest of is that, in the end, we came together as a team." He pauses and looks around the room. "Always keep in mind the power of teamwork, of compassion, and of your own will," he says. "I'm gonna miss you."

"We love you, T.J.," scream Pearl and Zoë, giggling.

I'm starting to get a little emotional. I can't believe I'm actually thinking this, but I'm going to miss this crazy group of people—well, most of them. I don't think I'll really miss the bikes, the long hot days of riding, or squatting down in the bushes on the side of the road, but I've never met people like this. I look at Pearl and Zoë. Maybe it's because they're older than I am, but they're just so crazy and nice and fun!

I take a deep breath and watch Brad as he steps up to the front of the crowd, his guitar hanging from the strap around his neck. "Before we sing our last round of our favorite song, we would like to present you with these very special Cat Island pins and your official certificates of achievement for completing this adventure."

Brad holds up a small pin. He squints at the tiny writing. "Courage, compassion, self-reliance," he reads aloud.

Everyone stays quiet while T.J., Brad, Katrina, and Tasha pin on the little gold Cat Island medallions and hand out the certificates. T.J. fastens a pin on my dress. "Always believe in yourself, Skye," he says, winking and handing me my diploma.

After a boisterous rendition of our camp song, the room fills with hugging and happy tears. People are choked up. It's emotional. Tasha is the first to hug me. "I'm so proud of you, Skye!" she says. "You made it!" I fall into her arms and soak up her great big hug.

"Thanks," I say before she moves on to Pearl, who's behind me. I scan the celebration and head toward the sofa, slipping by Katrina and Ian. I do not feel like hugging everyone. Just as I dart by them, I practically bump into Amanda. She's back in her black clothes, from head to toe, eyeliner and all. It's when we're face to face that I see it: the necklace, the one we gave her, the sea glass on the leather cord. She's wearing it around her neck.

For a few awkward seconds, we both just sort of stare at each other.

"Hey, congratulations," I finally blurt out.

Amanda fidgets with her long brown hair, like she's uncomfortable, too. I don't really know what else to say. I'm still having a hard time just forgetting about what she did and how she treated me. And I guess I don't think I *should* forget.

Amanda finally breaks the silence. "Maybe I'll see you sometime," she says.

"Yeah, maybe," I say, but really I'm thinking, *Right—maybe in a million years.* Even though I'm not scared of her anymore, there's something about her that still makes me leery. I guess when someone treats you like she treated me, it's not so easy to just pretend it never happened. I smile back graciously. "Good luck in school this year," I say, and I don't even flinch. I'm not tiptoeing around Amanda anymore. When it comes right down to it, I don't need for her to like me.

We both smile politely and turn to walk in opposite directions. I take three steps before I hear her.

"Skye," she calls back to me, reaching up and touching her necklace. "Thanks."

# CERTIFICATE
## OF ACHIEVEMENT

In recognition of successfully completing

## Cat Island Adventure Camp

Cat Island, British Columbia

## Presented to:

*Skye Beryl O'Shea*

*Moondog*

...ld "Moondog" Payson
...irector, King of Cat Island

CIAC

# Airport

It's still dark out when Tasha knocks on my door. "Skye, let's go. We've got to get a move on," she says loudly from the hallway.

I roll out of the most comfortable bed I have ever slept on in my entire life. It's still warm and so cozy. I want to stay in it forever, until I remember I'm going home today! I yawn, stretch my hands over my head, and look out the window at Kingfisher Bay shimmering in the moonlight. I walk to the bathroom and splash my face with warm water. Then I lather my face up with soap, rinse it off, and pat myself dry with the thick clean towels hanging beside the sink.

I slip out of my pajamas and jam them into the only bit of space left in my backpack. I squeeze into my jeans and throw my Super Girl T-shirt on over my head. Finally, I drag my two packs to the door and do a quick check under the bed and in the bathroom for anything I might have left behind. I walk quickly down the stairs, dragging my bags with one hand and pulling my hair back with the other. Ponytail in place, I stick Isabel's now-famous cowgirl hat on my head and hurry down the last flight of stairs to the lobby. Tasha, Zoë, Pearl, and Zack are already waiting sleepily in the van. We have the early flights.

At the airport, my flight leaves first. Pearl

and Zoë both hug me so tightly that tears well up in my eyes. But this time they are happy tears. "Don't forget to write, Super Girl," Pearl whispers in my ear.

After more good-byes from the rest of the crew, they deposit me with my return-trip flight attendant. Her name is Kai. I think she's Japanese. "Have a seat, Skye. I'll make sure you are all taken care of," she tells me. I collapse into a chair by the check-in desk, my day pack on my lap, and watch the planes taxiing around the runway until they call my flight. Kai escorts me onto the plane. "Let's see," she says, looking down at my ticket. "3A—you're right here," she says, pointing to the window seat in the third row back.

When they close the doors, nobody's even sitting next to me. After sleeping in a different place every night, the plane ride is nothing. It feels a thousand times different than my flight did three weeks ago. I lean forward and gaze out the window. I can see for miles and miles. I look at all the tiny houses down below. The cars look like little toys and the swimming pools like blue jelly beans. I sit back in my seat and lean my head against the window. I think of Zoë and Pearl and how much fun I had at camp. It was tough—the hardest thing I've ever done in my

life. But it was the most fun I've ever had, too.
I feel like I've never felt before, like I'm stronger
—like I can fly.

# Home

I sleep during the entire flight from Vancouver to Pittsburgh. In Pittsburgh, Kai flags down one of those golf-cart thingies and we race clear across the airport to where the smaller prop planes depart for Ithaca. She ushers me out to the runway, where she hands me off to a flight attendant whose nametag reads *Nadia*. "Hey, Skye!" Nadia says. "Let's get you on that plane."

In the small plane to Ithaca, I can't sleep anymore. I'm so excited to be going home. Home! I have the biggest smile plastered on my face. *Maybe I should eat,* I think. I unzip my day pack and feel around for the apple I grabbed from the Tennison Inn's fruit bowl. An envelope falls to the floor. Puzzled, I retrieve it and hold it up to see what it is. *Super Girl* is printed in neat handwriting across the front.

*What's this?*

I tear open the top of the envelope with my finger and pull out a fancy piece of Tennison Inn stationery. When I notice the signature at the bottom, my heart leaps. I read fast, and as soon as I get to the end, I read it again and then again, until the pilot's voice interrupts me.

"Get ready to land, folks," he says cheerfully over the loudspeaker. "It's a perfect day here in the gorgeous Finger Lakes region. The temperature is eighty-three degrees. Enjoy your stay."

I finally exhale. I'm home.

## CAT ISLAND
## The Tennison Inn

Hey Skye,

By the time you find this note, you should be home or on your way home. Or maybe the note has been sitting in your bag for a long time — whatever!

I just want to tell you that I think you're the coolest girl I've ever met. When I met you that first day in the airport, I liked your hat, and I remember you were the only one smiling besides me. You are really fun to be around, and you are easy to talk to, which is cool. It was fun to bike with you, and I will always remember the climb up Mount Tennison, the ride down, and all the crazy times we had on Cat Island.

So I guess that's it. I just wanted to tell you that I think you're really cool.

Your friend always,

Mason

Mason Grace
Lewiston, Maine
04240

# September

It's been one month since I've been back from Cat Island. It feels like forever. I'm going to just say straight out that everybody was right—my mom, my dad, the mailman, Tasha. It really was a summer I will never forget.

Ever since I've been back, a lot of little stuff that used to drive me crazy doesn't matter anymore. Now I don't think doing the dishes or taking out the garbage is such a major big deal. My mom says it's because I'm more appreciative since I've been through something hard. "You have perspective, Skye. Perspective is priceless." She likes to say that, and maybe she's right.

# Fate

The night before my first official day of seventh grade, my mom decides I need to go to this lecture with her. Of course she tells me that it's going to be really interesting and that I will love it. I do not want to go. I whine a little.

"Mom, I need to get my stuff ready for school. I need to figure out what I'm going to wear!" I say.

"Oh, don't be ridiculous, Skye. This is going to be *fascinating*," she tells me.

*"Fascinating,"* I say back, and we both laugh.

My mom and I walk the whole way to the lecture, which is at the university. It's about a fifteen-minute walk, which, before Cat Island, would have seemed like a big deal. Now it's nothing. The night is warm and pretty, and it still feels so good to be home. When we get to the lecture hall, there's a line going straight out the door, but my mom has tickets for the good seats, right in the front row.

I sit and wait until finally a guy appears onstage. He is really handsome. He sort of reminds me of T.J., but older. I sit up in my seat because I am three feet away from the stage and I don't want to be rude. The guy walks up to the podium and taps the microphone, making sure it's on.

*Thump. Thump. Thump.*

"Hello," he says. "The woman I'm about to introduce is an Ithaca native."

"Yeah!" shouts a person in the audience.

The man smiles and goes on. "She has grown to become one of the most accomplished female adventure athletes in the world."

*Hmmm . . . cool,* I think to myself.

"She has climbed the world's highest mountains, biked through rain forests in Borneo, run over volcanic rock in Hawaii, swum oceans in Australia, paddled rapids in Nepal—" The man smiles really wide and looks down at me. I sit up straight and smile back. He keeps talking. "*National Geographic* and *Outside* magazines call her one of the best female adventure racers in the world." He pauses, looks out at the audience, and smiles. "Please welcome my wife, Jade Odessa."

The crowd cheers wildly as this woman walks out onto the stage. She's strong and really striking. There's something about her . . . she looks so familiar. When she smiles out at the audience and her eyes sparkle and her face lights up, it hits me.

The Goddess—from the plane! The one who held my hand on my way to Vancouver.

I sit spellbound as she talks and shows slides of her adventures. When the lights go down and pictures beam onto the giant movie screen, everyone gasps, including me. I have never seen mountains that big or seen anyone dangle off cliffs that high.

"Maybe you'll do that someday!" whispers my mom. *Maybe I will,* I think to myself. After the talk, as everyone applauds, I tell my mom the whole story about the plane, about how Jade made me feel not as nervous, and about how nice she was to me.

"Wow! That's fate," says my mom, genuinely surprised.

When the clapping stops and crowds of people flood the stage, my mom actually lets me wait and try to say hi. We stand in the back of the line waiting to talk to Jade for twenty minutes, until my mom breaks it to me that we can't stay any longer.

"Please?" I beg.

"Skye, we've got to get home," she says. "It's getting late."

"Mom! *Pleeeeease?*"

"Sweetheart, you have to get to sleep. Your first day of school is tomorrow, and I have an early surgery shift at the hospital. There will be other opportunities." She turns to walk toward

the back exit. And, OK, I will admit here that
I am pouting and whining and displaying a little
bit of my pre-Cat Island attitude.

"I can't believe you made me leave!" I say
when I finally catch up with her.

My mom is not moved. "Don't start, Skye,"
she says calmly as we descend the stairs toward
the back loading-dock exit.

"Whatever," I say.

And it's weird, but the very moment when
I finally give in and follow my mom down to the
basement hallway, it happens.

Jade and Tan Man are right in front of us!

"Hey there!" says Jade, reaching out to give
me a hug. I hug her back, relieved that she
remembers me from the plane. "How was your
adventure?" she asks.

"Awesome," I answer, a little starstruck.

"Wonderful!" says Jade. A crowd of people
start coming at us from the other end of the
hallway.

"Honey, we better go," Tan Man says.

Jade turns to me. "That's so great. I had a
feeling you would make it with flying colors!"
She reaches over and puts her hand on my
shoulder. And just like before, her hand is warm
and strong, and when she touches me, it feels
like she fills me up with courage and strength.

"Hey, what's your name, anyway?" she asks.

"Skye," I tell her, still in shock that she is who she is and that this is happening to me.

"Cool name. Great to see you again, Skye!" Jade turns and begins jogging to catch up with her husband.

"Nice to see you, too!" I holler back. I turn to find my mom. That's when I hear her—it's Jade.

"Hey, Skye!" she calls.

I stop walking and turn to look back. A crowd of people flock around Jade, waiting to get her autograph.

"Always remember . . ." It's noisy and hard to hear her. I stand on my tiptoes.

"What?" I shout back.

"Sky's the limit!" she says, smiling brightly.

And now, more than ever, I really believe her.

# Adventurer Wows Sold-Out Crowd

**By Jay Greenberg, Tribune Reporter**

Ithaca native and professional adventure racer Jade Odessa wowed a sold-out Statler Auditorium crowd last night on the Cornell University campus. Odessa, 33, inspired the standing-room-only crowd with tales of her travels around the world, including her recent World Cup Eco-Challenge victory in Borneo and her world-record climb in Nepal. Next up, Odessa will lead a team of female adventure athletes up Bhutan's 23,997-foot peak, Chomolhari, which is known as "the mountain of the goddess." She will also hike through western Bhutan's Paro Valley on an ancient trading path.

Noel Jansen and his family traveled from Trumansburg to hear Odessa speak. "I've seen her on the Discovery Channel and ESPN, so I wanted to hear her in person," Jansen said. "She's amazing!" Eighty-two-year-old Gainy Brooks of Lansing agrees. "Jade's climbs are remarkable," Brooks said.

When asked which, of all the places she's traveled, she liked best, Odessa told the audience, "It's the journey, not the destination. No matter where I go, I learn that lesson again and again." After traveling to Bhutan, Odessa will join a group of scientists and explorers on a Russian icebreaker en route to the Antarctic Peninsula.

If you enjoyed Skye's the Limit!, take a peek at Skye's other adventure, Yours Truly, Skye O'Shea.

# Team Spirit Day

Just as we planned last night on the phone, Isabel meets me on my back porch at 6:50. We quietly sneak up into the bathroom before my sisters are even stirring. Isabel brings the special black hairbrush her mom got her from Japan, plus two hair ties and her blue plaid pajama bottoms. I run to my room and change out of my plain gray sweatpants and into Isabel's plaid pj's. They fit me perfectly. I slip my blue and gold Comets jersey over my head and take a quick look in the full-length mirror on my closet door, admiring myself before I run back to the bathroom for our hair project. I put the lid down on the toilet and sit facing Isabel, who quickly goes to work brushing out my thick brown hair, dividing it neatly into sections.

Isabel braids my hair into six different rows in the front and pulls the rest back into a ponytail. As soon as she's finished, she lets me sneak a peek in the mirror, but then we have to rush so we won't miss the bus. I wolf down a bagel and gulp some orange juice. We both grab our backpacks and run all the way to Kyle Kimber's brick driveway.

Everybody loves my hair. "Cute!" Paige says when I sit down next to her on the bus.

"You're so lucky to have Isabel as your neighbor," Olivia says enviously. It's true. I'm totally lucky. Even I have to admit that my hair looks really cool. My jersey is a hit, too. In front of our entire homeroom, Ms. Hahn asks me when our first game is. I am kind of embarrassed and kind of not, because I sort of feel like a celebrity.

At the end of school, Paige is waiting for me at my locker. I throw everything in my bag: science, social studies, language arts, and math. I'm in such a rush to leave that I almost don't notice the small, tightly folded note that is jammed in the vent of my locker door. I glance around to see who is watching. Paige is busy flirting with Cole Olson, whose locker is next to mine. The note is folded into a compact little triangle and wedged tight into the vent. I tug it slowly, being careful not to rip it on the sharp edges of the metal locker.

FOR SKYE O'SHEA #17

"FOR SKYE O'SHEA #17" is written neatly in black marker on the face of the triangle.

I begin to have major heart palpitations.

I have never gotten a note before, unless you count the notes Paige sends to tell me how bored she is in study hall. I have a feeling this note might be something different.

It looks like boy writing.

I turn and glance over at Paige and Cole. I quickly decide to open my mysterious note in the privacy of my very own room. I drop the note safely into the top pocket of my backpack and zip the pocket shut.

So who's writing Skye these mysterious notes? And how will she deal with her great-at-everything sisters, her impossible math tests, her crush on Ashton—and all the other craziness that makes up life at Lakeview Middle School? To find out, read *Yours Truly, Skye O'Shea*, available at bookstores and **americangirl.com**.